THE
COLLECTION AGENC
FILES

Previous books by Michael Mirolla

Paradise Island and Other Galaxies (Exile Editions, 2020)
The Last News Vendor (Quattro Books, 2019)
The Photographer in Search of Death (Exile Editions, 2017)
Torp: The landlord, the husband, the wife, and the lover (Linda Leith, 2016)
Lessons in Relationship Dyads (Red Hen Press, 2015)
The House on 14th Avenue (Signature Editions, 2013)
The Giulio Metaphysics III (Leapfrog Press, 2013)
Berlin (Denia Press, 2013)
The Ballad of Martin B. (Quattro Books, 2011)
The Facility (Leapfrog Press, 2010)
La logica formale delle emozioni (Edarc Edizione, 2010)
Light and Time (Guernica Editions, 2009)
Berlin (Leapfrog Press, 2009)
Interstellar Distances/Distanze Interstellari (Il Grappolo, 2009)
The Formal Logic of Emotion (Signature Editions, 1992)

THE
COLLECTION
AGENCY
FILES

MICHAEL MIROLLA

EXILE
e d i t i o n s

singular fiction, poetry, nonfiction, translation, drama, and graphic books

Library and Archives Canada Cataloguing in Publication

Title: The collection agency files / Michael Mirolla.
Names: Mirolla, Michael, 1948- author.
Identifiers: Canadiana (print) 2023043973X | Canadiana (ebook) 20230439780 |
    ISBN 9781990773181 (softcover) | ISBN 9781990773198 (EPUB) |
    ISBN 9781990773204 (Kindle) | ISBN 9781990773211 (PDF)
Classification: LCC PS8576.I76 C65 2023 | DDC C813/.54—dc23

Copyright © Michael Mirolla, 2023
Book and cover designed by Michael Callaghan
Typeset in Baskerville, Modern No. 20, Garamond, and Minion fonts at
    Moons of Jupiter Studios
Published by Exile Editions Ltd ~ www.ExileEditions.com
    144483 Southgate Road 14, Holstein, Ontario, N0G 2A0
Printed and Bound in Canada by Gauvin

We gratefully acknowledge the Government of Canada and Ontario Creates for
their financial support toward our publishing activities.

Canadian sales representation: The Canadian Manda Group, 664 Annette Street,
Toronto ON M6S 2C8 www.mandagroup.com 416 516 0911

North American and international distribution, and U.S. sales:
Independent Publishers Group, 814 North Franklin Street,
Chicago IL 60610 www.ipgbook.com toll free: 1 800 888 4741

To Jackie...
who I owe a far greater debt
than I can ever hope to repay.

TRANSLATOR'S INTRODUCTORY REMARKS
On The Finding Of The Files

*F*ollowing the collapse of the NatSoc Workers' Bank of Chicago Inc. in January, 2008 – an obvious victim of the subprime mortgage debacle, in combination with the usual derivatives and hedge fund mismanagement – and the subsequent seizure of whatever corporation assets were still in existence, the following items that have come to be known as THE COLLECTION AGENCY FILES (originally DIE DATEIEN VON DER SAMMLUNGSAGENTUR) were recovered. The materials, discovered among other documents and papers in safety deposit boxes within the bank's main vault, were originally in German and have been subsequently translated into English by the writer who accepts all responsibility for any errors of omission and commission within said translation.

Until 2019, the original items could be found in The National World War II Museum in New Orleans where they had been placed in secure storage under vacuum-seal conditions. The idea was to make them available for viewing by accredited scholars upon formal application (including this writer). This was done solely to protect the papers – considered valuable both as archival material and from the point of view of presenting some distinct vignettes from those troubled times, as well as unusual insights into the workings of what have been identified as several agencies active during this period – from further corruption and disintegration. However, it appears that not even these precautions could prevent the materials from being swept away by a combination of the flooding caused by Hurricane Barry and neglect caused by the on-going pandemic – and this after having survived Katrina.

The English translation of the items in question, five complete and one unfortunately in a very partial and fragmentary state, are presented below in the order in which they appeared in the original unbound manuscript as photocopied by this author. That order seems not to be chronological, but it was decided to leave them as they were found in the belief that is the way the original owners desired it. As for authorship, Items 2 through 6 are of unknown authorship, while Item 1 bears the signature of "A Good Soldier, S." However, even putting aside the obvious reference to Hašek's unfinished satirical masterwork, that authorship has been questioned by scholars (and I among them) for possessing a style and range of knowledge far beyond what would have been normal for a so-called "common soldier" ("Gemeinsamer Soldat") in the German Army of that period. As well, it is difficult to believe that the erudite "S." of Item 1, the lover of shells, poetry and fine upper-class ladies, despite his self-described malady, is the same persona as the hulking, brutish figure of Schweik that is met later on. However, unless new material comes to light (and that is very doubtful), this is a question that may never be resolved to everyone's satisfaction.

Please Note: For the purposes of historical accuracy, it should be pointed out at this time that, aside from the mention received in these papers, there is no other record of any organization with the name of DER SAMMLUNG-SAGENTUR having operated in Germany prior to, during and/or after the Second World War. There is thus the real possibility that these documents are purely fictional in nature, the invention of some fertile or febrile imagination looking for an outlet in times when other activities were extremely limited. If that is the case, there remains the question as to the purpose or rationale behind such a creation, in terms of what was to be gained by it; why this and not a more straightforward fictional narrative; or why it was felt to be important enough to bring across the ocean at the time of forced immigration.

In any case, whether fact, fiction or faction, the items do remain of historical value for anyone interested in that period in the evolution of the human social mechanisms that have brought us to where we are at present, and thus the writer/translator feels justified in offering them for general consumption by the public. The reader at that point may come to his, her or their own conclusions.

MM
January 20, 2022

ITEM ONE
AT THE WALL ~ A LETTER

Date: June 5, 1944
To: Berghof Haus, Berchtesgaden, Bavaria
From: Die Wand, Vierville-sur-Mer
Circulation: Private Files

*T*here are moments, Adolf, when one feels quite alone.
When there seems to be no one else in the entire universe. No doubt you have experienced much the same sensa-
tion on occasion. Perhaps when pacing the floor noiselessly at
the Eagle's Nest. Or waiting for an inspiration late at night in
the Bunker. Or hovering over strategic maps of the Eastern
Front at your aptly-named Wolf's Lair. But allow me to suggest
that yours is a different type of loneliness. And thank God. You
have many things to occupy and inspire you. Like the juggler
at a performing show who tosses up and keeps in the air an
ever-increasing number of multi-coloured balls. Or perhaps in
our case, only uniformly-pale-coloured balls of a blondish hue.

I, on the other hand, have little to occupy me but my
no longer shiny army-regulation binoculars and this ten-
centimetre slit in the concrete. Not that I wish to complain but
the engineers might at least have arranged it so that the slit
would appear at eye level. Or did they have in mind, when
planning them, the ideally eugenic man, blond, fair and six-
foot-four on coming to full attention? However, not to worry.
My finely-honed ability to adapt ... to improvise ... has

enabled me to overcome this problem and to thus keep a watchful eye on the ocean, the ever-present, ever-dangerous, and luminescently-tipped ocean. I have managed this feat (and you for one will appreciate the irony of this) through an ingenious use as footstools of tomes such as Spinoza and Freud – thick-spined monstrosities whose warpage is, on most occasions, more likely to be mental than physical.

But I exaggerate about the ocean and its dangers. It observes me more than I it. Given our unrelenting aerial attacks on our enemies across the water, what can these channel waves bring except more waves? And sand. The coarsest sand. Oh, we must not forget the crabs that scuttle sideways towards the barriers and occasionally fall in through the slit. They are fat and juicy and delicious over an open fire. I will send you some – crated nicely in ice – with the next mail pickup. They will go well with your *Liebfraumilch* and your tender Geli. Oh, I am sorry. I assume that should be Eva now, shouldn't it? We sometimes lose track out here so far from the nerve centre. From the living pulse of the nation. Like "A Message from the Emperor," (*Eine kaiserliche Botschaft*) is it not, sent "to you alone, his pathetic subject, a tiny shadow which has taken refuge at the furthest distance from the imperial sun"? But no death bed scenes, I would hope? You must remain strong for your vital fluid to feed and nourish the rest of us, even if it is a mere drop of that fluid once every hundred years for the least and furthest of your subjects.

Yesterday, after some of the heaviest rain yet, the bolt on the door rusted so badly it swelled and jammed shut. The dampness is such that I am constantly reminded by contrast of the *Hohe Alpen* in winter. There, pretending to be Hans Castorp himself but without his genetically-inherited pulmonary weaknesses naturally, I could sit on top of the world and breathe through my nose deeply and with little difficulty. Now – and again I do not wish to complain but feel these things must be recorded for future generations basking in the brilliant warmth of the eternal reign – I must be careful not to spray the walls of my cubicle when I snore … and snoring is one of the few pleasures left me.

Can anything be done about it? I fear not. Drops of murky water squeeze through the concrete as if it were little more than a sponge to soak in moisture. The drops slide down the walls and collect on the floor, forming rivulets and puddles. These puddles eventually darken with rust (as does everything in this accursed place) from the re-enforcement iron rods and soak into the propaganda pamphlets I use to keep the water from spreading to the foot of my bunk. After many tries, I managed to slide the bolt free (thanks in large part to a gift of petroleum jelly from a thoughtful friend back home who has been made exempt from military duty due to extravagant myopia and other less acknowledged concerns). But it was only after numerous jarring blows from my rifle butt that the door squeaked open – and then but a few centimetres. The rest had to be done with a large metal bar and required several of my companions for proper leverage.

I took the opportunity during a lull in the rain to step outside for some fresh air and a bit of stretching. Far out on the water, I glimpsed the flash of a deep-sea diver, his fins rising for a moment straight into the air before vanishing again beneath the tenebrous surface. Checking that the mines are in place and properly armed, no doubt. Even now, it's amazing to watch these creatures, no longer encumbered by umbilical cords, air hoses, and cast-iron suits, make the sea their own. Slick as eels. A small torpedo boat circled nervously around him, all hands on deck and ready with machine guns primed. We must beware of the underground (and the underwater). So we have been told. We must be on constant alert. Some, rumour has it, are still foolhardy enough to dispute our hold on the country, the start of our thousand-year reign. Hard to believe, I know, but again this far from the power nexus, dilution of faith and belief has to be expected. A dulling of enthusiasm in the daily grind.

Thus, the mines must be constantly watched, examined, and repaired. Foreign material is meticulously removed from their surfaces. Before the contact mines were replaced with the new magnetic beauties, many were the nights I was awakened by an explosion echoing lavishly within the bunkers. These bunkers are wonderful for echoes, you must know, much like the yodelling meadows of that traitorous so-called neutral country that we will swallow when the time is deemed right.

On such occasions, in the morning the sea would be awash with red. It brought to mind Lady Macbeth. I know you have a cultured imagination. Are you familiar with that particular allusion? At any rate, I made it my concern to discover what type of fish it had been before becoming a blasted-to-Asgard one. In order to shear off the bolts and detonate the mine, a certain minimum weight and momentum were necessary. Even then, the mine had to be rammed in a

very direct head-on way, almost deliberately. Like some stub-
born and determined salt water billy goat. It passed the time to
sit cross-legged on the sand and wait for the carcasses to float
in. In most cases, the fins were intact and the heads remained
in reasonably good condition – all things taken under consid-
eration. Some had their eyes and other organs replaced by
shrapnel while a large number suffered only from the subsequent shock waves. Most were sharks. More than that I have
been unable to ascertain.

But it is not from lack of trying. The books I requested –
and which would have greatly aided my research – are months
overdue. I would be eternally grateful if you could do something about that. Put the word in someone's ear. Or whatever
it is you do to help speed things along. In particular, *The Elasmobranch Fishes* by J.F. Daniel would come in handy. Yes, I know.
His monograph is in English. But sometimes one has no
choice. Sometimes one must remain language-neutral in these
matters – at least until the time when we can claim it as one of
our own. Soviet-style, yes? In everything from the automobile
to the Zeppelin!

But aside from that, aside from what are probably unavoid-
able war-time delays and thus to be tolerated if not forgiven, I
wish at this time to lodge a formal protest. I do not want to
trouble you with these sorts of things when I know you have so
very much on your mind these days. But in this instance, I feel
I must speak out. Not just for myself but for the greater nation
at large. The common good. The populace that forms the basis
of the societal pyramid upon which you stand at the pinnacle.
You see, a collection agency has been hounding me without

mercy throughout the war. Yes, can you believe that? It has been demanding payment for a mail-order belt with double-eagle buckle I sent away for several years ago.

Now, I would very gladly pay for such an item and just as proudly wear it. Except for one thing: It was never received by me. I thought I had straightened the whole thing out when I sent a note indicating as much. But they wouldn't believe me, saying the belt had definitely been sent and that I was reneging on a contract I had signed of my own free will. A contract they would be only too glad to show me. Again, I wrote back admitting to the contract but also pointing out the absence of said belt. And again, I received a form letter threatening the loss of my credit and other dire consequences if I did not remit the full amount within a certain time. At this point, I was understandably livid and sent them a note telling them in no uncertain terms where they could put the belt. And they could start with the pointed eagle-beak buckle!

Since then, strange men and even stranger women have followed me wherever I have been posted. They have hovered about just out of reach, just beyond the area where I could justifiably strike back at them. Or get several of my mates to waylay them and administer a good beating. Let them understand that I mean business. Money-lending thieves and poor excuses for human beings! But they are smart (perhaps "cunning" and "eel slippery" are more appropriate words) and, like a pack of wild dogs, make sure they have plenty of escape routes before launching one of their attacks.

Are you familiar with them? You should know that this agency is barbaric in its methods and with little sense of morality. Or dignity. I do not understand how we tolerate them in our midst. How we allow them to roam about without fear of reprisal. On one occasion, an Agent dared commit the atrocity of disguising himself in the uniform of the Fatherland – can you believe that? Don't they shoot spies for doing that sort of thing? He then wormed his way into the wall by claiming to be the military bed-bug exterminator. They are, by the way, a severe problem here. Bed bugs, that is. But his uniform didn't fool me. The Agent's, that is. I realized immediately he was a collection Agent and not a soldier because of his swarthy skin and hooked nose. And he wore glasses so thick you couldn't make out his eyes. Obviously, an inferior specimen. Or a case of unprincipled breeding. The type of character that has managed to slip through the genetic net – at least thus far, and obviously unfit for military duty. Fortunately, my pay voucher hadn't yet arrived or I might have given it to him simply to get him out of my sight.

After several minutes of pretend inspection and fake hosing down of my bunk, he came right out and accused me of not paying my debts to society. Then he held out an ID card – a gold-embroidered card, imagine! – and pushed it right up against my face: "Claudius, Chief Collection Agent. No Debt Too Small; No Debtor Too Large." I laughed at him, then yelled that the problem of bed bugs could be solved by putting metal posts on the bunks rather than the wooden ones in use. That would give the Agents … sorry, I mean the bugs, no place to hide. He made as if to protest, saying bed bugs were the least of my problems and that being in arrears on one's debts was akin to treason. But I reached for my rifle and he ran out, dropping pieces of his disguise in his wake, including a rubber nose and pair of glasses.

The last I saw of him, he was scrambling up the beach, much like a crab, and shaking his fist at me. He shouted something about the nerve of going shopping full well knowing I wouldn't be able to pay for my purchases. And something about re-instating debtors' prisons for the likes of me. I aimed the rifle at him yet he slipped further away. He continued to shout but, owing to the wind and the waves, I couldn't make it out. He did, however, point to the sea and make what seemed like exploding actions with his arms. Then, in an act of pure madness, or so it seemed to me, he pulled off his own belt and swung it around several times. That was the last straw and I opened fire, forgetting for the moment that these Agents are under the special protection of the *Schutzstaffel*. But by then he was too far away and only a very lucky (or unlucky) shot would have brought him down.

The closest I came to catching one of the scoundrels (it may actually have been the same scoundrel, come to think of it) was outside a church in Nice while I was stationed near that city. Decadent and unwholesome, by the way. Filled with sleazy watering holes frequented by low-class whores and squint-eyed rats and weasels on two legs. If you want my opinion, a city best razed and started anew from the ground up, quadrangulated to make the marching of armies easier. My mates and I were emerging from just such a slop house in the early dawn when I spotted the villain. I must have caught him unawares and was almost upon him, brooding as he seemed to be over some ledgers, when he happened to glance up. He did a double take as he recognized me, then immediately turned, looked about, and ran into the nearest church, a place he probably thought would serve as a sanctuary.

"I have you now," I said, rubbing my hands and ordering one of my fellow soldiers to go around the back to make sure he couldn't sneak out that way. "You're trapped! Scurvy weasel!" I shouted. "And I'm going to give you a thrashing to within a centimetre of your life."

With another of my mates at the front entrance in case he attempted to step around me, I followed him in, certain that all escape routes were blocked and that I would soon flush him out into the open like the skunk that he was, stinking up our Fatherland with his demands for payment and compensation for products that were never received. However, once in the church, he seemed to have vanished into thin air. The only person that I encountered when I stepped in was the priest in charge, a mealy-mouthed fellow with a sickly smile and teeth that were too good for him. Holding out both arms, he welcomed me in and wanted to know, smiling in that disgusting fashion all the while, if I had come to confess, as it was that hour of the day. I ignored his brazen insults and asked him instead what happened to the person who had come running in before me. He looked around in bewilderment and shrugged his shoulders. In effect pretending not to know anything about it, despite the fact I had found him standing at the door and thus he could not have possibly missed the person running in.

I then began marching about the aisles of the church, up one row and down the other, yelling all the while that only the most despicable cowards hid behind the skirts of religion, even one as misguided as the Roman Catholic Church. But the priest, that popish knave, again holding out his arms as if in blessing, kept on insisting I had been the first to come in that evening and that, if I did not believe him, I was most welcome to look around. Or to search every nook and cranny, if I so desired. "Nook and cranny" were his words and they described the inside of that church very nicely. The Agent could be hiding anywhere and it would take an entire troop to flush him from whatever rat hole he'd found – and probably with the help of this sickly smiling sycophant priest. I yelled again that he was a coward and, with a last plunge of my bayonet into the confessional, prepared to walk out.

"Bless you, my son," the priest said, making the sign of the cross.

"Bless me!" I yelled, pushing my face practically up against his. "Do you know who you are harbouring here? These are the scum of the earth! Bloodsuckers! Soulless creatures without an ounce of patriotism." I paused, took several breaths, and tried to calm down somewhat. "Bah! But then again what do you know of patriotism? What do you know of defending your country against the enemy? Bah! I might as well be talking to a rotten tree stump."

"All our fellow creatures, friend or foe," he said, glancing up to the sky as if waiting for approval, "are deserving of forgiveness and understanding."

"Fine words," I said. "Very fine words. But you'll be singing a different tune, let me tell you, Father ..."

"Er ... Laudamus ... Father Laudamus."

"You'll be singing a different tune, Father Laudamus, if … no no, not if … *when* … when they ever get you in their clutches. A different tune altogether when those leeches start to suck you dry. Take the very marrow from your bones."

"I'm a poor parish priest," he said, fingering the rosary hanging from his waist as if that were proof of his abject poverty. "What would anyone want of me?"

"Oh, they will find something. Mark my words." I wagged my finger at him. "And then you'll be sorry you harboured this … this scum … this … this … *canker* … this yellow pus on the nation's otherwise unblemished flag … this … this …"

As I stood at the front of the church and searched for more ways to vilify, feeling myself once again heating up beyond all reason, I saw another priest come out of a bakery and walk towards us, carrying several of those thin anorexic breads barely enough to feed a child of five. (*No wonder these Frenchmen offered so little resistance*, I thought.)

"I must see to my parishioners," Father Laudamus said, turning suddenly to re-enter the church.

"Remember what I said," I shouted after him. "They don't care about God, religion, patriotism, the Fatherland, the family … They only care about collecting debts …"

The other priest approached, whistling softly to himself. I noticed he sported the same rosy cheeks, the same imbecilic, mealy-mouthed smile. Do they come from an assembly line or something? The Silly Priest Imbecilic Smile Assembly Line? Emerging from somewhere in the bowels of the Vatican, that gaudy snake-pit.

"Greetings, my son," he said. "A fine day."

"Morning, Father," I said, touching the side of my cap. "Your friend awaits you. The two of you can spend the day smiling together. See who cracks first."

"My friend? Smiling together?" He tilted his head like one does when quizzical. "I'm sorry. I don't follow you."

"You don't follow me?" I said. "The other priest."

"The other priest?"

"Yes, the parish priest," I said, pointing towards the church. "Father Laudamus, I think he called himself. Not too bright, I don't think. Just come from the priest farm, eh?"

"Well, young man," he said, with that stupid smile and crinkling of his eyes. "You must be mistaken. I'm the parish priest here. Père Allemagne. In fact, unless this Father Laudamus has suddenly descended from on high, I'm the only priest here. War time rationing, you know. We are spread quite –"

"Son of a bitch!" I yelled, turning to run into the church, followed by my two mates. "Son of a two-timing whore-monger!"

But it was too late. The so-called priest was gone. Vanished into the slimy back streets. Leaving only discarded vestments behind, folded neatly across the back of a pew. In my excitement, I had forgotten all about their incredible ability to disguise themselves. To slither in and out acting like genuine human beings.

"Son of a godless bitch!" I repeated, allowing it to echo throughout the church. "One of these days … one of these days, I'll catch up to you. And then …" I drove my bayonet into the nearest pew, impaling a missal. "The end, my friend. The end."

15

There must be something you can do about these life-draining leeches, Adolf. Perhaps pump them with fresh blood and serve them up as sausages at one of your diplomatic dinners. Or drop them over our enemies. Anything to keep them away from the populace. They should not be allowed to distract your loyal and long-serving warriors from the task at hand. We who are on the far edges of the Reich cannot afford to have our attention diverted from the cause, cannot afford to let the barbarians slip through for momentary lack of vigilance. Especially when those barbarians are already in our midst. Bad enough to have to keep an eye on those coming from across the waves. And who knows what the long-lasting effects of such activities will be on our illustrious nation. They eat away at our shared goals and purpose, at our coming together. They separate us from the herd one at a time and emasculate us, undoing the sense of manhood we've tried so hard to build up through Wagner and Nietzsche. Yes, you must do something. Your imperial duty, if I may be so bold.

A confession. A tiny confession. When I spoke earlier of being alone, I wasn't entirely truthful. You are the first to know that I do have an occasional visitor. In fact, it was she who saved me from despondency and useless rage after the collection agency incident. We met over shells. Literally bumped heads, as we both stooped to pick up a particularly beautiful specimen of *Babylonia spirata*. I deferred to her, of course, both out of Teutonic chivalry and the fact these are not particularly rare in this part of the world. Since then, we have become intimate and she comes to the wall once or twice a week. She has told me nothing about herself but – by the way she walks, by the clean and perfumed silk garments she wears beneath her military-cut coat, by the professionally-styled hair and manicured nails – there's no doubt she is a lady of some standing. And, though she removes the ring before entering my little cubicle, the mark gives away her marital status.

What she sees in a common soldier I can't fathom. But she insists, saying I'm not at all common, that I represent the best the Fatherland has to offer. I do not argue, especially when she orders me to lie on my bed, proceeds to straddle me wearing only her stiletto-style high-heeled boots and my eyes are clouded over by a certain indefinable feeling of blissful eruption spreading from my groin. Ah, Adolf. Afterwards, she thanks me profusely and walks out, head held high as if daring anyone to say anything, and her boots echoing on the concrete steps leading out of the bunker area. I do not at any time question my good fortune for fear of having it all vanish as nothing more than a childish dream, one of those where we awake – and I can tell you this, man to man – all wet between our legs.

Speaking of wet, the weather this year has been singularly atrocious, and one hardly knows it is almost summer. It is not all bad, however, for it allows me to ease the weight on Spinoza and Freud, which seem to be sinking, shrivelling, the words mashed together in even more confusion than normal for such prevaricators and obfuscators. No match for Nietzsche, beyond a doubt. And, while the waves roar and the winds blow, the Fatherland may rest easy with its home fires burning and tiny perfect potatoes roasting on the rosy-cheeked coals. Poseidon himself would think twice before launching an invasion. It seems the gods, or at least a good portion of the more northerly ones, are on our side, does it not?

I find it an appropriate time, while lying in my bunk, to read poetry. It keeps my mind off the scummy water and the bed bugs, who are simply waiting until I doze off before commencing to feast. You are fond of poetry and even write some yourself, do you not? So I heard. And that is good. After all, what is a man without culture? How else can he repel the bombs and bullets of savages and inbred barbarians except with carefully selected poetry?

Yes, I am well-provisioned against invasion. One needs not this thick concrete wall riddled with steel bars. Nor the row on row of cannon buried in rock with only their muzzles projecting. One needs nothing but Schiller and Goethe and Heine with perhaps a deft pinch of Wagner to send the mind soaring and the enemy reeling, unable to attain such heights, unable to reach where we have so effortlessly climbed with hardly a loss of breath. I have taken the opportunity while here to write a little operetta which I trust will please and entertain you. It is modestly titled *Freude zu Kultur*. The music is light and pleasant, almost airy, while the lyrics are in the style of that traitor, Herr Brecht, an easy mark for parody. My protagonist is Kultur who, dressed in a blue suit with knee-length sailor pants, blithely walks along the sea with the water washing his milk-white ankles while off-shore bulldog batteries shell him without mercy and star-striped sharks snap at him. All to no avail. The idea came to me in a dream, though I must admit to having altered it slightly. Originally – and I feel I'm safe in telling you this without fear of it going any further – Kultur was being shelled from both sides. Doesn't make sense, I know. Only goes to prove how unreliable the subconscious can be and what an idiot that other quasi-Austrian was for relying on its revelations.

As you can see for yourself, all would be almost idyllic if it were not for those bootlicking Agents and this hereditary disease of mine which seems to erupt, to mushroom as it were, in damp places. No one knows of it – except my lady visitor who finds it … er, stimulating – and I trust your discretion in the matter. There are some I could mention, malicious and unscrupulous, who would take advantage of this unfortunate condition to prevent my advancing and achieving my proper station in the course of the thousand-year Reich. These are the ones who wish to twist wonderful Nobel Prize winner Herr Carrel's words about the taking of "energetic measures against the propagation of the defective, the mentally diseased, and the criminal … humanely and economically disposed of in small euthanasic institutions supplied with proper gasses." I am thinking in particular of the collection Agents and their ilk as fitting this description, don't you agree?

Ah yes, the other matter: my ailment. My slight genetic defect. To be brief, I suffer from a disease of the skin known as hirsutism or hypertrichosis. There is no cure. Fortunately, it only manifests itself in extremely damp and humid places where there is a lack of sunlight. It starts with my back and buttocks (and this is almost a permanent state now given the hyper-dampness). It spreads from there to my stomach and shoulder blades, to my arms and legs, so that they become matted in spots like the floor of the thickest jungle. It seems as if, scrub as I might, I find myself permanently dirty.

19

Finally, given enough time, and if I remain too long within the bunker, it makes its appearance on my face, covering it entirely save for my eyelids and nose. This is not usually a problem for me because I make it a rule to step out of my damp quarters at least twice a day: first thing in the morning after waking, and last thing at night before going to bed. My pelt quickly recedes in the open air, becoming once more a thick black patch at the base of my spine just above my buttocks, just itching and twitching to explode again.

However, I was recently laid up for two weeks (only a slight broncho-pneumonial infection, no need for concern or get-well cards), unable even to lift myself off my bunk. One cannot imagine the horror I felt on seeing my face for the first time after at last acquiring the strength to get up. I had to look twice at the cracked piece of mirror before recognizing myself. My face was buried in thick, curly hair, the features slowly receding in Neanderthalic waves. I quickly turned away, feeling nauseated and disgusted. What had I done to deserve this? Had we not staked all qualities of virtue and vice on appearance? And rightly so. For what else is there but appearance, ya? What does having a pristine soul really mean? How can anyone tell if not from the external presence and look of the person's face? How can swarthiness ever translate to purity of spirit? After all, is not purity represented by whiteness? Has it not ever been thus? From the earliest reports in *Die Bibel.* I looked around me and all I saw was blackness. Darkness. Greasiness. Dare I say it? Werewolfishness.

Nevertheless, there must be those who do not judge from appearances. Or perhaps, they judge all too well. What Proust, the old reprobate, would have called an "inversion." For instance, my visitor seemed peculiarly galvanized into action when she dropped in right in the midst of my illness and spotted my naked body lying on the bed. Quickly shutting and locking the door behind her, she came rushing towards me, flinging off clothes with reckless abandon, rubbing her fingers through my hair, her face against mine, taking delight in watching my tongue slither out of a bushy hole towards hers, and telling me how much she enjoyed the caress of coarse hair on her … ahem … female parts.

At the same time, she suggested I do various unmentionable things to her, to her vulnerable and exposed body, things she said her husband had once mastered but had long since forgotten in his desire to save his energy for more public orgasms. I refused firmly, telling her that no common soldier should go where an officer feared to set foot. Or other parts of himself. She stormed out in a huff, leaving me even further depressed. I should perhaps have not been so precipitous in my refusal. After all, even common soldiers get certain dispensations, do they not?

But once I stepped out into the open air (carefully, of course, so as not to let anyone else see me under such conditions), the world seemed a much brighter place again and I was able to face my comrades without shame. Still, I must be on my guard against any laxness in this matter, especially where my visitor is concerned. For she is, as I have already stated, a great lady. One need only look at her immaculately polished, plush leather high-heeled boots and wolf fur cap to realize that. Have I mentioned those boots before? Well, if so, it doesn't hurt to repeat it: her ability to negotiate her way along the stones and sand of the beach atop those boots represents the epitome of Germanic/Teutonic womanhood. No match for your Eva naturally but in the same constellation beyond a doubt.

You will be pleased to learn that, despite our distance from the imperial palace, there are plenty of portraits of you. In fact, each bunker has one or two nailed to the wall. However, these are mere two-dimensional representations, likenesses that do not capture the fullness of your personality and magnetism. Thus, as there is an abundance of clay and water here, I have decided to put my skills to work and create a definitive sculpture of your features in bas-relief. Yes, I knew that would further please you, as does all praise from the common man. For, not to be too modest about it, it was the common man who first saw your promise, even in the most unwholesome of surroundings and awash in beer barrels. It was the common man who elevated you onto that tavern table, was it not?

I'll model the sculpture after the description in *Philhellene* by Cavafy. Have you by any chance read this poem? Of course, I realize you are a very busy man, but I feel these verses are especially appropriate for what you are trying to achieve, for the way you perceive the world around you as something malleable and there to be shaped, no? Here, let me quote it for you: *Be sure the engraving ... [Seien Sie sicher der Stich ...]*

On second thought, this must sound very presumptuous of me, daring to teach you, of all people, about poetry. You probably know *Philhellene* by heart, read it over and over again as a child when you first became conscious of your manifest destiny. You must forgive my over-anxiousness, my over-didactic

nature. In any case, I will send you the completed sculpture –
along with some letters my visitor has asked me to forward –
with the next regular courier.

Speaking of letters, we do not get much news any more at
the wall. Come to think of it, we have never received much
news here, at the furthest talon and claw, the most remote
grasp of the empire (now that the Eastern Front is no more).
The enemy wishes to take advantage of this by showering us
with pamphlets in our own language – atrocious word-by-word
translations, mind you, but still readable. I mention this last
because I have never given much credence to rumour and propaganda. But one must know one's enemy to fight him well,
don't you think? You must have seen them, yes? The pamphlets, in the lowest of Low German, speak of unspeakable
atrocities supposedly committed by our glorious troops in the
course of the fighting, the march across vast expanses and con-
quered nations.

They speak of millions – yes, can you believe it, millions –
not just of men, but also women and children – murdered
while naked and helpless, of tortures and experiments that will
never see the light of day. And they even have the nerve to provide photographs of these alleged atrocities. How desperate
and silly can these barbarian rabble-rousers be? Do they think
the world so naïve it can be fooled into believing that a nation
such as ours, steeped in centuries of culture and poetic sensi-
bility, in Norse purity and the windy reaches of Valhalla, could
do such things? No, the words, the photographs condemn
them, not us. Their falseness is obvious from a purely logical
viewpoint. Still, they have gone to much trouble, to great pains

in an effort to discredit us, have they not, Adolf? We must do the same to them.

And this is where I would like to make a modest proposal, one that would serve to solve several problems all at the same time. I propose that we discard a part of ourselves that has proved disgusting and underhanded, a part of our society that has undermined all that we have worked for throughout the many centuries during which our culture has been built. I truly believe that, if we can cut away this dead and rotting burden, we will rise even further in the esteem of the world. We will be able to dominate others with the simple lifting of an orchestral baton. Or a masterful novel. Or those latest new-fangled movie reels that our darling Leni has put together so well. We will become unstoppable – not through superior weaponry (although that always needs to be there in the background, ready to respond to threats from those who are perverse enough not to appreciate our culture and refinement), but through the sheer power of what we represent, what we stand for, the pinnacle of earthly creation and existence, the summit of eugenics and genetics, the perfect combination of brain and brawn. The one true everlasting superpower ready to declare the end of history, fist wrapped in glove.

But in order to reach these heights, I must re-iterate we need to discard a part of ourselves that some unfortunately have come to see as one of our defining points. A part that has become practically encrusted around our souls and is slowly sucking their life spirit out. Yes, I am speaking of our bureaucratic tendencies. It is amazing how the fierce Teutonic poet and warrior would come to be identified with those who sit by the thousands at desks in cavernous offices and spend their days dotting and crossing, keeping track of the movement of cattle cars and gas ovens and such arcane and mundane things. Or the workings of lawyers like grubs, insinuating themselves into the very heart of governance with their lip service bow to so-called justice. This is not the image we want to present to the world – at least not if we hope to arrive at the type of conquest that force alone can never achieve. No, we must re-engage our poets and warriors, our spirit of adventure and our pride. We must find those who are prepared to do battle when the time comes, when the gods come calling: "And from their spears / the sparks flew forth."

How do we do that? How do we re-invigorate our nation in a time of obvious crisis? Well, Adolf, I am very happy that you asked that. Most extremely glad. I think I have a proposal that will not only elevate our Fatherland but also cause our enemies much confusion and turmoil. Will sow the seeds of discord in their midst. Will give them a taste of their own medicine. And it is something that can be very easily done once we put our minds to it. Something that does not require huge amounts of materiel or personnel. Something that is simplicity itself, if I say so myself.

I propose we put those scumbag traitors on a ship and let it float out to sea. Let them drift upon the oceans to land where they might but hopefully on shores where they can spread their particular virulent disease far and wide to the point of debilitation, ruin and wrack. But it must be done now while the war is still being contested. It must be done while the energies of the enemy are focused elsewhere. It must be done while the fog remains in their eyes and while their blood is overheated. Else, they will quickly catch on and turn them back, keeping the epidemic from their shores.

Who, I can hear you asking? Of whom do I speak? Who are these carriers of pestilence and perdition? These destroyers of art and culture? These fifth columnists ready to take apart the very fibre of a society strand by strand?

Why, the collection Agents, of course. Can there be others imbued with more perfidy? Others more dangerous? Others more ruthless?

I Remain Your Faithful Servant (With Sharpened Bayonet)
A Good Soldier S.

ITEM TWO
THE DEBT ~ A MEMORANDUM

Date: November 10, 1942

Author(s): Unknown (High probability of attribution to [a] Collection Agent[s])

Circulation: Internal/Collection Agency Executive Committee

*T*he Collection Agency – whose motto "No Debt Too Small; No Debtor Too Large" was not long ago respected and feared throughout the civilized world as emblematic of law and order has fallen on hard times. The once-powerful influence of its Agents is scorned and despised by the very people who should fear it most. We are referring to the debtors, of course. Wherever they go in search of debt recovery, the Agents are greeted with derision and thumbed-up noses. Doors are slammed in their faces with alarming regularity; night pots are unceremoniously tossed on their heads; giant dogs are allowed to clamp on to their legs and masticate to their hearts' content.

Claudius, a master of disguise and one of the most valuable Agents in the field, has even suffered the ignominy of being forced to resort to physical violence against a recalcitrant debtor. In more normal times, he would have been dismissed on the spot – or rather, he would have considered himself released from service the moment his fist struck the debtor's face. Nay, the moment he thought of it. And no excuses allowed. Instead, he escaped with a severe reprimand and a new assignment in occupied territory – the unenviable task of collecting debts from soldiers at the Western Wall. He was saved from further repercussions by the assaulted debtor's patriotism which prevented him from cluttering up the courts while so many treason and espionage trials were being processed. Nevertheless, the Agency has had to surrender all hope of recovering the money he owes. It paid the client, an American boot and helmet supplier for the elite corps, out of its own already over-extended pockets.

Even in these uncertain times of changing tactics and unexpected violence, of fifth columnists and total war, the Agency prides itself on one outstanding virtue – scrupulousness, followed closely by strict honesty and a desire to have everything debit/credit balanced out perfectly when the war comes to a successful end. It has the government's tacit permission to do this. But the populace as a whole, and those who owe money in particular, seem to think that this war is simply an opportunity to unilaterally cancel their debts or to reduce them according to some obscure laws of wartime inflation related most nearly to anarchy. The return of the Jacquerie in front of the Bastille, no doubt. Or the filthy rabble in Petrograd.

Bills sent by the Agency are used as napkins and toilet paper. (There is, it must be confessed, a genuine lack.) Or as score sheets on which to mark the results of Skat games. Thousands of accounts return with *forehand / middlehand / rearhand* scribbled across them. Agents are turned away with the plea (the excuse) that the country is at war and rationing takes all the money. Or that no one is buying flowers anymore so the business is going bankrupt and how can one then repay the vase maker. That sort of thing. What have we come to when mothers stand in doorways with their big-eyed children and plead with the Agent to give *them* money? The most insidious of all are those who claim that being drafted exempts them from debts. There was a time when only officers made such high-handed claims. But now even common foot soldiers are getting into the act, with several Agents barely escaping with their lives while on legitimate missions to recoup such debts. And all at a time when money must be made to flow more freely if the economy is to remain liquid and stable, with the ability to absorb the inevitable shocks of war.

Many debtors are also incorrigible hoarders, unwilling to part with the gold and silver coins buried in their backyards, where they languish uselessly just when they are needed most. How else, argues the Agency, is the country to repair old weapons and obtain new ones for the defence of the State? What else will keep the trains running? The planes flying? The ships steaming? Daily, lucid and persuasive tongues wag in the ear of the Minister, asking for a definitive policy that will end the Agency's degradation and give it the powers it needs. The difficulties of the situation are readily appreciated, the Minister says. But his hands are tied. The wheels within the wheels of bureaucracy are slow in churning. Even if that bureaucracy is largely a creation of the Agency in the first place. These things, unfortunately, have a tendency to gain a life of their own, with the children no longer responding to the proddings of the parent.

But, make no mistake, this does not mean that the Agency is slackening its vigil. At the Agency's headquarters on Freudestrasse are kept the records of every single debtor in or out of the country, from a Pfennig owed to millions of Marks, from chimney sweeps and failed artists to manufacturers of steel and ice cream cones. The files are complete down to birthmarks and aliases and are kept up to date by a battalion of trained clerks who work like tireless monkeys, sleeves besmirched with ink. Soldiers and secret police surround the squat, imposing Romanesque-Gothic edifice. One look at this practically windowless structure should be enough to convince most sane people the building is impenetrable. But already two attempts have been made to destroy these records.

The first still leaves people whistling and shaking their heads. Here is an inter-office memorandum (memoranda are a popular form of communication within a bureaucracy), from one high-ranking Agency official to another, describing the scene:

"I was just about to put the finishing touches on a very satisfying case – a case involving traitors as well as debtors – when the fire alarm sounded within the building. We were filing out the door in an orderly fashion when the first fire truck screeched to a halt in front of us. Smoke already poured out in thick columns from the upstairs window next to my office. I feared the worst.

"The firemen ordered us out of the way and aimed their hoses at the window. Suddenly, rather than abating, the fire raged out of control. Flames seemed to shoot from the hoses themselves and leap against the building. None of us noticed at the time, being too busy looking at the fire, that these hoses were connected not to a hydrant on the street but to a tank on the truck. Fortunately for the Agency, the real firemen arrived in time to undo some of the damage done by the gasoline fired under pressure into the building."

The pseudo-fire truck tried to rush away but was blocked by tanks and personnel carriers that just happened to be in the area. The perpetrators who survived were quickly arrested, had all possible information extracted by unpleasant but necessary means, and then executed after *in camera* tribunals. The Agency still has that much influence. Before they died, the name of the man who had started the wastepaper basket fire and then pulled the alarm was pried out of them. He turned out to be one of the Agency's most trusted operators, responsible for the northern sector of the retreating Eastern Front.

At first, the Agency was at a loss as to why such a man would take such a risk, given as he was probably set for life, including a home in the Baltic Sea Usedom Island resort village of Heringsdorf and a hefty pension following retirement. A thorough investigation revealed that he had bought a fur-lined wolf cap on credit years before and had forgotten to pay the bill – or it had been lost in the mail. Now that he was reminded of this fact, probably by coming across his own name in the Agency's files, it was too late. He was already listed among the deadbeat debtors and no amount of money could erase that. He feared (with just cause) the loss of his job and any subsequent pension when the Agency finally tracked him down through the use of its extensive cross-filing system. Nor could he be consoled by the fact that his death (by firing squad) would end his sorrows. He knew very well that this would simply mean the passing of the debt to his wife. She, much to her credit, paid promptly and so only has the husband's black mark in her files.

For a short while after this incident, the Agency regained a great deal of its pre-war influence, so much so that rumours were soon bruited about among its enemies of it having started the fire for that very reason, having already previously discovered the Agent's forgotten debt. Money from debts small and large poured in and was quickly funnelled into the war effort – better magnetic mines, desert tanks, chemicals, rocket and atomic weapons research.

Some records (debtors Caarlt to Cruyden) were destroyed in the fire but, before these people had time to rejoice, the Agency used its brief moment of glory and clear lines of communication to announce that duplicates were kept in the steel vaults deep below the building. This is not strictly true (requiring too much space) but was done for the good of the country. Now, the debtors Caarlt to Cruyden will never know and must dread, like the rest of their ilk, the end of hostilities and the return to fiscal normalcy.

The second attempt was simply a pathetic try on the part of the debtors to gain the country's pity. Several thousand mothers, dressed in their oldest rags and covered with fake sores (could they be anything else with the advent of free medical care and clinics at every street corner?), marched to the Plaza on Freudestrasse and started to hurl rocks at the building. The police were instructed to let them do as they wished – a certain level of tolerance is desirable and besides they could do no damage. But the mothers mistook this generosity for weakness. Several squatted on the building's marble steps (a gift from an enlightened ally in Italy) and proceeded to defecate on them. Others writhed on the cobblestones, giving the impression that the tandem of poverty and debts had reduced them to such a pitiable state.

The order was given for the police to disperse them before enemy spies were able to get photographs which might prove detrimental to the moral fibre of the State. The mothers, not for themselves but for the sake of ideal motherhood, were treated with kindness and gentility. What's more, boots were parachuted on to them so that the sores on their feet wouldn't get worse. None of this, however, was enough to convince the most militant of the mothers to disperse and, in the end, the police were forced to fire upon these recalcitrants with the resultant loss of life.

The war has caused problems within the Agency as well. Any able-bodied man who becomes an Agent is immediately exempted from the draft. At the start, since the Agency has always had difficulty with recruitment, it accepted anyone who displayed a willingness to do the work, especially since the rolls of the debtors have skyrocketed. But it was soon discovered this was a mistake. Many of the Agents turned out to be second-rate, unable to adapt to the changing times and useless for the task at hand. Others have become involved in criminal activities, accepting kickbacks to alter the files, lending money out on their own at exorbitant rates verging on the usurious.

Recruitment had to be stopped altogether and a thorough evaluation of the existing personnel conducted. Only recently, having cleaned out the stables, has the Agency been able to restore its much-coveted internal balance and to get on with the task for which it was created.

How does the Agency work? The best way to explain is to take an example from its current files, as there is no rule of confidentiality. In fact, the more exposure a case gets the easier it is for the Agency to embarrass a debtor into paying up and to convince the next debtor that it means business. Let us choose a file that will not arouse the misguided sympathies of bleeding hearts on both sides of the conflict. Item: A diocese in Nice owes the Heilig Book & Ecclesiastical Supplies Co. of Buenos Aires (through a branch office in Dresden) fifty Marks for the purchase of a Bible, several missals, a dozen hymn books, and one gold-plated chalice.

A simple and straightforward transaction, involving a purchaser who can definitely afford the products, its coffers replenished like clockwork on the seventh day. However, the account has been outstanding for more than three years. Every effort by the company to contact the diocese has proved unsuccessful with letters being returned unopened. On the one occasion when the company does receive a response, it is in the form of a sermon denouncing money changers and usurers and signed 'Père Allemagne' – at the time believed to be a pseudonym designed to evoke feelings of patriotism; later discovered to be this person's actual name. With many regrets but having no choice, the Heilig Book Co. turns the account over to the Collection Agency and agrees to a standard provision whereby the Agency receives fifty per cent of any debt collected outside the country.

Three separate Agents, two from Nice and one from headquarters, are dispatched. The three work in tandem yet independently of each other and one will not know if and when one of the others has collected the debt until it is reported back to the main office. The first Agent from Nice is assigned telephone duty. It is his task to call the rectory every day of the week, and perhaps several times on Sunday, to remind this Père Allemagne of his duty – at least to Caesar if not to God. The second Agent sits at a mahogany desk and composes polite missives. He makes veiled allusions to 'practising what one preaches' and the fact that the gates of heaven are nothing but needle-eyes not only to rich men but also for those who are loaded down with outstanding debts. These two Agents are chosen not only for their obvious abilities but also for their extreme politeness. The first phone calls and letters consist of the most innocuous generalities and pleasantries. No direct mention is made of the debt. The priest is given to believe his conscience is pricking him and everyone knows how fond priests are of conscience and its pricks.

Here is a typical telephone conversation between Agent One and Père Allemagne, one fairly late in the game:

Hello. Père Allemagne? It is I. And how are you today? We spoke yesterday –

35

Sir! Whoever you are, my patience is running thin. You must stop disturbing me during my preparations for Mass. There are people waiting for my blessing, waiting to communicate with God. This is most serious.

Terribly sorry, Father. My sincere apologies. We must respect the sanctity of Holy Mother Church at all costs. Don't you think so?

Yes, yes. Absolutely. Now, may I ask what is it you want? May I help you with something?

Throughout the ages, the Church has withstood attack after attack because its leaders were men of exceeding faith and honesty. Is that correct? Dignity and humble pride have characterized both its martyrs and its dealings with even the least important of its members. It has been a towering pillar of strength –

Sir! Is it all right if I give the sermons around here? I am the ordained priest, after all.

Again, my apologies. To presume your task on my part is inexcusable and unnecessary. Tell me, Père Allemagne, do you listen to confession?

Of course. That is, after all, my God-given right and it must be exercised on demand. Even you must be aware of this, no?

You're right. How stupid of me! Utterly imbecilic. Tell me this, Father. You must hear plenty of nauseating things, I bet. Hidden vices, cankers of the mind, disgusting evil committed under the cover of darkness, real or symbolic, or behind the veils of well-regulated and adjusted society. You must hear plenty.

I do. But what I hear is strictly confidential and I am there to forgive not to pass judgement. You must excuse me but –

Is it possible to confess over the phone?

What?

You know, over the phone. Can you forgive someone across telephone wires or must mouth to ear contact be made?

Now look here —

How idiotic of me once more! Won't I ever learn? What a time to start a theological conversation, eh? Why, I imagine, many of these very things are now being discussed in the Vatican — or is it Avignon? — under the cloak of infallibility. They are ex cathedra without the Pope's imprimatur. Or is it anathema? At any rate —

The Agent's extreme politeness and unwillingness to get to the brutal point, coupled with a genuine but side-tracking interest in Church matters, is rewarded consistently by the slamming down of the telephone. If it is Sunday, he will call again and the conversation will be repeated with but slight variations. Agent Two might at the same time be composing a letter such as the following, keeping flies at bay with his free hand:

Cher Père Allemagne,

As a man of God, you know better than anyone the consequences of allowing a state of war to break down all lines of communication between people, all attempts at normalcy. At that point, society collapses in an unholy heap, n'est-ce pas? That madman Jean Jacques Rousseau's perverted theories have a chance to re-assert themselves and be proven disastrously wrong all over again with a resultant loss not only of individual life but also of culture and breeding. Enlightenment, indeed! As a man of God, it would be up to you to restore those lines as soon as possible, would it not? The best way to do this is to maintain an air of normalcy. Don't you agree? Banks must keep on banking. Jails must remain locked. People must cling to the social virtues such as honesty, good will, and faith in other men.

These are difficult, even perilous, times. Without honesty, goodwill and the co-operation of others, we are in danger of losing our perspective. And what is life without perspective? Take, for example, the people's attitude on debts during a war. It is immoral and not pleasing in the eyes of the just God. An eye-for-an-eye God. He recognizes, as I am sure you do, that refusal to pay debts here on earth can lead only to greater evil, to the wages of sin. These same people would make light of their debts to God — if it weren't for the promised retribution — just as easily as they do those they acquire on earth. And then they complain that the war is filled with atrocities, prisoners being brutally murdered, women and children strafed on roadsides, churches bombed. Why? Why is that? You know the reason, Père Allemagne. You know.

A Conscientious and Honest Friend

Finally, there is the fallen star himself, Claudius, straight from his humiliation and punishment at the Western Wall and eager to redeem himself. Having volunteered when he heard the debtor was none other than Père Allemagne, he has the task of 'confronting the debtor cleric face to face,' in the priest's own backyard, as it were. After studying the situation for several weeks and noticing that it is a bright, sunny day in Nice, he decides the time is right. He dips into his ever-handy trunk and pulls out the front of a vestment, a vestment he has used many times before and made for easy application and removal. Carefully, he applies a touch of black eye shadow to accentuate his ecclesiastical stare, some rouge for that apple-cheek shine, and then a hint of lipstick (just a hint) for good measure, to bring out the youthful bloom and sweet innocence favoured by clerics.

Of course, Claudius and Père Allemagne have crossed paths before. Well ... almost crossed paths before. But Père Allemagne is not aware of that. He is delighted to greet a fellow cleric, even though Claudius has disguised himself as a Spanish Jesuit while Allemagne is an ardent Franciscan, practically sworn enemies in more normal times. But the finer points of theological controversies can be put aside, as they would be in the meeting in the desert even of a Christian and a Muslim, for instance, with one carrying food and the other water – and neither armed.

The two sit beneath a grape trellis, in the comfortable shade of the rectory courtyard, commenting on the terrible war and the beautiful weather. For some reason, Claudius has taken a liking to Père Allemagne: There is something about him that is pleasant and down to earth and that puts those in his presence at ease. But, at the same time, Claudius senses that a cloud of some type hovers over Allemagne's joy, threatening to dim it. He sips his iced tea and stares out towards the tree-lined boulevard, the almonds and chestnuts in full blossom. His preoccupation is so intense he forgets to sweeten it with the customary two lumps and his face twists into a grimace.

"There is something the matter, Father?" asks Claudius, his eyes brimming over with a kindness and concern that he almost gets himself to believe is more than simply his job, simply part of the act.

"I beg your pardon?" He reaches down and drops three lumps of sugar into his tea. "Oh, no. Nothing important enough to burden your thoughts with, Father. Just the trials and tribulations of war. Of the times, don't you know."

"Yes, a shadow of uncertainty has fallen over us all. The creatures of the earth who once walked upright have now reverted to four legs again, to the hunter and the hunted. A sad state, however necessary it may turn out to be in God's long-term plans." The faux-Father Claudius lowers his eyes for a moment before lifting them again to look with concern into Père Allemagne's face.

"But I see more than that in your expression. I see personal problems, immediate difficulties, troubles involving private matters. To sum up: Worries of a non-spiritual nature. Am I correct?"

"You are most observant," Père Allemagne says, nodding. "Most astute."

"Yes, I've been told that more than once. The Jesuit in me, I guess. Can I help you with them? Is there anything I can do to ease those worries?"

"Not only most observant but also most kind." He shrugs. "But it is nothing. Really. Or rather nothing that you can help me with."

"Perhaps it would be best to speak of it to someone else. Sharing, as our Saviour said, is half the answer. Remember we were admonished to go set the world on fire. And to find God in all things. No matter how trivial." He places a hand on Père Allemagne's knee, squeezes it gently. "Besides, you should let me be the judge of whether I can be of help or not." He pauses and looks around. "Or is it something that is better dealt with by your confessor?"

"Oh no," Allemagne says, shaking his head vigorously. "Nothing like that. Nothing of the sort at all."

"Well, then," Claudius says with a quick smile, a tilt of the head, and a jocular attitude. "Out with it!"

"You know, Father." He sighs, his chest heaving. "I haven't known you for very long. But you might be right. You might be absolutely right. It might just be for the best."

"I'm certain it is."

Allemagne leans back, looks up at the sky and then towards Claudius.

"I don't know where to begin," he says, clearing his throat, "except to say that I can't understand one bit of what is going on. For several weeks now, I have been receiving … what best can be described as mysterious phone calls … and strange letters."

"Threats?" Claudius asks in a whisper and looking around suspiciously. "The secret police perhaps? They have been known to move in inexplicable ways, you know."

"Oh no." Allemagne waves his arm and laughs nervously. "Nothing of the sort. More in the way of general discussions on morals and ethics and man's duty to man. Always very considerate and polite. Although lately I have started to discern a note of personal vindictiveness. Also, the telephone caller never stammers or loses his train of thought. He might just as well be reciting a part of the Litany."

"I see," Claudius says, sipping the last of his tea and placing the cup on the table between them. "Hmm. Do they perhaps want something from you?"

"I've considered that," says Père Allemagne, scratching his chin. "But what on earth could they possibly want? What could they want from me? I am a poor man, a servant of God, with little money to my name. Even less now that His Holiness the Cardinal has left the country for an extended pilgrimage to Argentina. I once had a small vineyard in Provence but that had to be given up when I entered the priesthood. This grape trellis is all that's left of it. My only possessions are a Bible and some tattered missals. And even these have become the common property of my flock."

"Perhaps they feel you have done something wrong, something for which you must pay. Is that possible?"

"Well, then, if that's the case, why don't they come right out with it?" Père Allemagne is becoming somewhat irritated. "Why don't they confront me face to face? Are they so unpalatable they must hide behind mysterious phone calls and letters? Are they so evil the cloth of the Lord frightens them off? I am a patient man — one must be in times like these, our country enslaved and our people serving another's will — but even Job doubted for a moment — and I am no Job."

"Judge not lest ye be judged in turn," Claudius says, starting to really get into character. "Is your past so unblemished that you can say with all conviction … without the least doubt … they have no legitimate grievance against you? Have you always been fair in your treatment of others? In your business dealings? Is there nothing you regret?"

"I am no angel, Father. Only a priest. I have erred, committed many indiscretions, on occasion coveted—"

"More tea, Father Allemagne?"

"What?"

"I said, do you want more iced tea?"

"No, no. My cup runneth over as it is. Once, in my youth, I even blasphemed. That was the moment I realized my vocation. And pride – that's the hardest part to bear."

"Biscuits?"

"Sorry?"

"Biscuits! Biscuits! Are you deaf, Père Allemagne? Can't you understand your own damn language?" He jumps up, making his chair tip back and the jar of tea rattle on the table. *Perfect*, he thinks. And then, the pronouncement: "Pay your debts or roast in hell, you miserable hypocrite!"

With that blessing, Claudius stalks away, tearing off the clerical vestment as he goes and tossing it aside. It settles on to a rose bush, impaled on its thorns. He stops and turns toward Allemagne: "Damn hypocrite! Traitor to the Fatherland!"

Claudius smiles as he turns away again, prides himself on having carried it off so well. But at the same time, he feels a twinge of regret at having to abandon such a pleasant companion. Père Allemagne, on the other hand, is completely shattered. The brimming glass in his hand shakes all the more as he tries to steady it. Ice-cold tea spills over his shirt and seeps quickly to his skin, chilling the flesh unpleasantly. With his free hand, he spoons lump after lump of sugar into the tea, then swallows the paste in one gulp. Several hours later, he is still sitting there, horribly disoriented and unsure of not only where he is but even who he is. During this time, the telephone in his rectory rings almost continuously.

Among the numerous virtues which endear the Collection Agency to its clients is the tenacity the Agents display in their pursuit of debtors. Often it happens that the client has all but given up hope of ever recovering the money. Only to receive a letter in the mail with a cheque for the amount owed, minus the Agency's commission. In many cases, the letter is returned to the Agency with a note that said business no longer exists. Factories and manufacturing plants are obviously prime targets during a war. Many of the Agency's clients have already been blown off the face of the earth. Others can not wait for the debts to be collected and quietly go into bankruptcy, the owners themselves becoming debtors.

But the Agency has an inviolable pledge, and this pledge is answerable only to itself. In the case of Père Allemagne, that notorious disciple of chaos and social disorder, every Mark collected from him (totalling one hundred fifty with interest) goes towards an improving of the war effort since the Heilig Book & Ecclesiastical Supplies Co. of Buenos Aires, Dresden Branch, is now a cemetery for bombing casualties. Père Allemagne himself, more responsive than most to the prod-dings of conscience, mysteriously attacked a priest who came to visit him, a certain Jesuit by the name of Girasol. His action has been attributed to shell shock, a bomb having exploded dangerously close to him as he sipped his tea one late afternoon. The incident serves nicely to set off an inter-nal squabble between the Franciscans and the Jesuits, of which only the iceberg tip is visible to the layman. Needless to say, the slightest spark is all that's required to heat up these centuries-old internecine religious wars. Once out of the desert ... and armed ...

⁂

On a more elevated level, the Collection Agency is once again pressing the government for more rights and powers. How long will it be possible to keep the Agents from acting in the same manner as the debtors? They are spit upon and have chamber-pots dumped on their heads. At night, Agents must walk through the streets in pairs. Already several have been brutalized and maimed for life, forced into premature retirement at great cost to the nation. Their home addresses must be kept strictly secret. Especially now that the march of the mothers has failed and the anger of the truly ignorant must find other outlets. Claudius is only one example of what might happen, for it is the finest, the most conscientious Agents who suffer most. They are used to better times and successes like Père Allemagne are few and far between these days.

The Agency is not asking for much. First, it wants the right to search suspected homes without the need of a warrant, which in times like these might take months to obtain. Besides, dozens of other agencies − secret police, spy networks, special investigators, the SS − are given priority when it comes to warrants. Or can already perform their tasks without the clumsiness of warrants. Secondly, the Agency pushes for the right to allow its Agents to carry weapons. The almost daily threats to life and limb can no longer be ignored. In anticipation, strict rules have already been set up within the Agency to regulate the use of these guns and even stricter penalties are in store for any Agent who violates them. Finally, every Agent should be empowered to seize property on the spot, merely upon proof that the person is indeed the debtor in question – and it should be any property owned by the debtor and not only the item or items in question. Given these powers, the Agency has promised – war or no war – to reduce the debts of this nation to an insignificant trickle. Even if this means such a successful campaign that the Agency must eventually disband for lack of work.

ITEM THREE
The Realpolitikal Reform ~ An Example

Date Released: July 21, 1944
Author: Unknown
Circulation: Ministerial/Governmental/Collection Agency Executive
   Committee
Type: Event Summary

*T*hanks to an anonymous tip from a woman who claimed she wished nothing save to serve her country, a courier has been intercepted with startling consequences for all involved. At first, it was believed he acted simply as a minor spy in those largely ineffectual networks that spring up like weeds during a war. They uncover material of the greatest importance right after Herr Goebbels appears at a news conference to announce it. Or they walk straight into the traps set by our ever-alert interior ministry agencies, thus providing information to the enemy that is false if not detrimental to their war effort.

However, no one could have suspected, when they shot the courier trying to flee through the Ardennes Forest, the significance of the letters he was carrying. Nor could the lieutenant in charge be blamed if he couldn't read what was in those letters. Naturally assuming the papers were in code, he did the right thing and handed them over to the district SS man. He, in turn, had them sent – under armed guard – to the main de-codification centre back in Berlin. But no matter how much the words were tortured and distorted, converted to numbers, added and subtracted, or run through mechanical decoding systems, they stubbornly refused to yield up their secrets.

That they were decoded at all could be considered an absolute stroke of luck – if it hadn't turned out that the Collection Agency was involved. What happened was that one of the menials, a swarthy fellow whose job it was to pick up and incinerate waste paper at the centre, glanced at a pile of sheets on a desk and read: *Plans For A Shadow Government.* That he could do this while dozens of others had failed is easily explained. He had been a scholar of ancient Greek languages previous to the war before academia was cleansed of his sort. And not just any ancient Greek languages but that of what is called "Linear B," spoken in the Late Bronze Age. When the demand for these types of Greek scholars quickly waned, he'd put himself on a list of those available for government service. The Collection Agency recruited him, bonded him for security reasons and then, in order to have their own man at the decoding centre, had found him this job.

Naturally, as soon as the top echelon officers were told of his serendipitous discovery, the man was ordered jailed. For his own good, of course. But, when the military police came for him, he had mysteriously vanished. Or rather, the Collection Agency had re-located him within the filing-cabinet bowels of their headquarters, as close to sanctuary as could be found and much safer than any church. The officer in charge of those sent to arrest him was informed of this after the fact and assured that he'd been sworn to secrecy so that no word of the plans would ever leak out. Language experts with the highest security clearance were then called in to finish the translating task. Here are the results:

∞∞

Greetings Cleisthenes,

If the time was ripe yesterday, it is over-ripe today. You have indicated the people are with you all the way. Beware of them. It's not seemly to have the mob at your back. When they strike, they can't differentiate friend from foe. Remember the Revolution of 1789. Of course, the desire of every popular leader is to mould the rabble [rubble] to his image and likeness. You have done that admirably. So admirably perhaps that some of the more intelligent are now asking themselves what it is that distinguishes you from them. Oh yes, even here along the sea and so far away, we hear of the turmoil and upheaval brought about by your agitation. Is it true there are now roving gangs of perfectly respectable middle-class burghers who become political monsters at night, attacking the secret police and Collection Agents and tattooing their foreheads? Much of the glamour would be lost if it became widely known that these are spontaneous outbursts. Take the blame for them, at least in the eyes of the underlings. The small risk you run will be more than compensated for when our larger plan is unveiled.

My transfer here has done little to aid my marriage. We are still as far apart as ever. I am attracted by the bright lights of the nearby town and the music that floats to us. The women there are all smiles and seem hungry for men, chocolates, and cigarettes. Most of their husbands and lovers are either dead or in the underground with little

*chance of surviving the war. She, on the other hand, passes the time
collecting shells and playing with Rollo. He, like me, is becoming
more frisky with age and has turned into the most fantastic specimen
of a purebred German Shepherd. If only people could be bred with
the same purity and taste for obedience.*

*As for my wife, I don't know what to make of her. Two days ago, she
cut herself on the wrist with one of her confounded shells. Not too deeply
but just enough to bleed profusely and put a scare into all of us. Fortunately, one of the soldiers from the wall spotted her and was able to rush
her for medical treatment. I owe him her life. She is resting at this
moment. I have so far refrained from asking how it happened for fear
she might disclose the truth. She is a sensitive creature, as you well know,
and not made for these robust and goose-stepping times. Her mind is
constantly on Romantic poetry and Goethe.*

*As well, I think she is carrying on an affair – perhaps Platonic,
perhaps not. And, with whom, I have not been able to discover. But she
sometimes comes home at night smelling of another man. It doesn't matter to me as I have other concerns. But there are dark moments when I
tire of her affectations, her long lonely walks on the beach, her sighs and
moans, moments when I wish to break her in two. But then I'm afraid
two of her would grow back to haunt me ever more.*

*Nevertheless, we are both looking forward to seeing you here with us.
Perhaps your boundless humour will serve to revitalize her or at least
restore her complexion. Have you ever noticed how Romantic poetry
blanches a person and drains them of blood? I, myself, am more healthy
and active (in all ways) than ever. My strict diet and strenuous daily
exercise have served me well. You will be no match for me in tennis or
swimming. So, remember that mind and body must work as one. Our
nation must be trimmed of its fat and excess baggage, the creamy*

madness rising to the surface to be skimmed away. What better people to do it, eh, old friend?

In Keeping The Oath,
Lycurgus

ॐॐ

My dearest Solon,

The choice for our Pericles can no longer be in doubt. As much as I admire your legal experience, knowledge of jurisprudence and punctilious adherence to the letter of the law, I don't believe – and here you must concur – the people will accept you as their leader. The nature of your work has kept you entirely out of the spotlight. As well, you are too honest and not a good enough actor for the role. Dissembling is a major part of a successful politician's repertoire. No, there is only one man who qualifies, who fits the bill. A natural leader. His past is spotless. No atrocities or unnecessary butcherings stain his record. No incriminating images of back-alley deals with shady characters wearing low-brim hats over their eyes are being floated about. Although he is aristocratic by nature and family background, the role of popular hero suits him well. I, among many, am convinced he is exactly the man needed to pull the disparate threads together and to prepare our nation for an honourable peace. Or as honourable as it will be possible to negotiate at this perilous moment in time.

As well, he has acquitted himself admirably throughout long and difficult military campaigns, a fearless patriot despite his intense dislike for certain members of the inner circle. Even today, with our backs literally to the wall, it is important to keep our martial prowess at its peak and not become another nation of shopkeepers (though *confidentially that nation has done well for itself). Only tactical errors and failures in logistical planning have prevented us from further conquest. And further conquests are now out of the question – at least for the foreseeable future. However, if we are to maintain what we have earned, this insanity, this dark tumour, must be expunged from our midst. For a nation with our history, our culture, our refinement, the status of being a pariah is out of the question. We must at all costs and for the sake of civilization re-establish – if not our supremacy – at the very least our legitimacy within the brotherhood of nations.*

Needless to say, Solon, you will play an integral part in all this. The shape and scope of our future laws have been left to you. As we have experienced to our detriment, nothing is more important than a system of checks and balances, a way to keep any disturbed, narcissistic, power-mad and paranoid individual from stealing the nation from under our very noses. The time will come, much as we dread it and find it difficult to stomach, when the reins of government will fall once more into civilian hands. Your laws and the nation's willingness – nay, desire – to obey must, of necessity, cement that process. No figurehead role for you. Absolutely not! You will be remembered as the father of a new spirit in this soon-to-be-made-great-again nation. In this moment of impenetrable gloom, I can see the ghosts of our philosophers, our politicians, our scientists, our poets, our musicians, our artists and our military leaders amassing behind us, holding up the true banners of honour, civility and enlightenment.

I beg you not to overly concern yourself with the lawlessness currently holding sway in our cities. We are merely fighting fire with fire. Let me remind you of our schoolboy days before you left the Academy. You once complained – do you remember? – that no one fought fairly any longer, but you were determined to do so. Until the day one of the nouveau riche bullies kneed you in the groin and left you gasping for air. There's no need for me to go any further. My wife sends her utmost regards and an inquiry as to whether you might not obtain the latest edition of Schiller's Complete *for her. At the same time, I eagerly await the first draft of your laws.*

 Yours in Trust

 Lycurgus

⚜

My Glorious Pericles,

 There is still time for you to re-consider your position. That you did not give your assent on the spot can only be attributed to a lack of information, a lack for which we must take the blame. But no longer is it possible for you to plead ignorance of the situation or claim that your distance from the maelstrom lends enchantment to the overview. While in the midst of battle, with the sand in your mouth and enemy fire on the horizon, such beliefs are understandable. After all, there are more important matters to occupy one at these times. I know, having myself fought in a cleaner war — a cousinly spat — when the honour of the nation was indeed at stake. But now we have presented you with considerable proof of what the present regime has done to degrade our race in the eyes of the world: the separation and imprisoning of innocents; the use of state assets for personal gain; the debauchery and degrading of our womankind. A war, as you well realize, is no time to discard all concepts of fair play and decency. History is especially harsh when it comes to treating these matters. If we are to kill men and defeat nations, let it be done with pride and dignity. Butchers are nothing but specialized shopkeepers and no better than house painters who don't realize their place in the scheme of things.

The government in power has descended to such depths that not even high-ranking army officers are immune from insult and embarrassment. Only last week, a retired general and personal acquaintance of mine was shoved by the mob on the street. Then, when he took out his ceremonial side-arm and started to shoot — over their miserable heads, mind you, he was arrested. The main culprits in all this are the Collection Agents. They have had the nerve to hound my wife for over a year, demanding payment for certain silk undergarments she had bought on a whim and then no longer desired, handing them to a waitress who allows me to glimpse them on occasion.

No one seems to have the authority to liquidate them once and for all, wiping their bland smiles and hangdog looks from the face of the earth. In fact, reliable sources have informed me they are on the verge of receiving tremendous new powers — powers of search and interrogation, powers to carry weapons, etc. Are we to believe they are simply Agents collecting debts? Ridiculous! A more reasonable assumption might be that the government is using them to gather information, to spy, and eventually to take over the duties of the secret police. A combination of bookkeepers and torturers! A throwback to those dear Franciscans.

These Agents must be stopped before the new powers are granted them and they become untouchable. Intimidation and scattered assassinations as in the past are not enough. That would only serve to make them popular. Besides, the Agents themselves are concerned solely with their duty. Excellent soldiers, in other words, who can easily be re-trained to serve a less rabid master. As well, we have already attempted to destroy the Agency itself without much success. It is too well-protected, kept out of the line of fire by someone very high up in the hierarchy.

We must have the people behind us, and you are the man for this. Without a doubt. Already, and this is in the strictest confidence, we have turned down Cleisthenes (too much of a rabble-rouser and lacking the support of the army) and Solon (too intellectual, too technical, and unable to deal effectively with common-sense matters). They will make unparalleled lieutenants in any case. I offer my humble services as well, along with the modest resources at my disposal. Nothing will be required of you in the initial stages except your approval of the plan. You are absolved of all bloodshed or involvement in any needed terminations. The people must come to recognize you simply as the soldier who did his best, with honesty and courage, against insurmountable odds. Your natural modesty and infinite good breeding will take care of the rest. Of that you can be assured.

The taking over of the government by you will guarantee democratic elections the moment the war comes to an end. How can we possibly deny the people their rights? Most have served the nation well, giving their lives without question for what they believed to be the greater good. Is it their fault this has proven untrue, has resulted in a series of lies and atrocities leading nowhere? They have only rumour and hearsay to guide them, whispering of attempts to make the nation great again. Most do not possess the necessary schooling and intelligence to understand the reasons behind a war, the vast movements of history and the inevitable clash of ideas. Are we to blame a hungry, desperate, angry populace for clinging to the filthy skirts of the only man who seemed able to feed them, clothe them, give them dignity?

Even I feel a twinge of remorse at having to put this prosperity at risk. But I am willing to live with it. Remorse might well be the greatest and most practical of all attitudes in the eyes of God but also the least useful when it comes to human affairs. My wife is always saying

how terribly sorry she is, how terribly sorry for being terribly sorry.
Even a confirmed atheist finds delight in conquering remorse when
committed to the lesser of two evils. You, personally, need not concern
yourself with this. Simply be prepared to take the reins of the riderless
caravan. That alone is enough to win you eternal fame. Or eternal
satisfaction, if fame is found too fleeting.
  I Remain Strictly Confidentially Yours
  Lycurgus

Next is presented the infamous document itself, known as
Plans For A Shadow Government: Prelude and drawn up jointly by
the three who called themselves Lycurgus, Solon and Cleisthenes (with any input from Pericles as yet undetermined):

We advocate a return to the Greek city-state, as yet unde-
cided between Sparta and Athens with influence from
Corinth definitely minor. The neo-Spartans among us favour
a curtailment of decadence and the destruction of all night
clubs, bars, taverns, and other locales of debauchery – which
they feel is where the current evil festered. Perhaps to be
converted into gymnasia for the improvement of body and
soul. Or barracks. The entire country is to be placed on a
strict diet until such time as deemed sufficient to reduce
bloated bellies and sharpen dull minds. No extravagance of
dress or behaviour shall be tolerated either in private or in
public. Under pain of death. The pan-Athenians, mindful
of human frailty and temptation, ask only a labelling of
prostitutes according to their talents and abilities. Also, they
want a demerit system for people who live beyond their

means, who frequent night clubs, bars, taverns, and such like places too often and who dance instead of concerning themselves with intellectual argumentation. The pan-Athenians have the upper hand at the moment, but the final decision will rest on the people.

We advocate a war tribunal with all-encompassing powers to come into effect immediately upon the cessation of hostilities, regardless of victory or defeat. Information has been leaked that the enemy is planning just such a tribunal as a display of international justice. To show them the extent of our good faith, we should beat them to the punch by trying our own leaders and generals both for war crimes and for tactical errors, with punishment escalating as errors shade into crimes.

The present caretakers of this nation have much for which to answer, and we intend to see that they do. As well, we seek the immediate disbanding of the Collection Agency, that perfidious society of psychotics whose only purpose is to harass innocent citizens. We have accumulated file upon file on this Agency. Neither secret police nor palace guard has acted so cruelly and barbarously towards its own people. Once the Agency has been disbanded, its Agents are to be integrated into the new military.

A total reconciliation with the Church is also deemed advisable, particularly by the neo-Spartans. Already several of the country's Archbishops have been discreetly approached. We have the Vatican's tacit approval for our plans, in return for certain favours including state funds for re-building and re-structuring. After all is said and done, it has been found that religion is still the easiest and most affordable way to draw people together both before and following a war ... as long as the members of the First Estate are aware of where the power actually lies.

As to the economy and the serious matter of inflation, we propose the immediate sale at the highest bid of our top scientists to foreign powers with an abundance of wealth but a paucity of technological know-how. These scientists have worked feverishly and unquestioningly for us throughout the war, making us the leaders in armaments, advanced battle techniques and human experimentation and eugenics. They would be only too pleased to do the same for any nation that adopts them and pays them handsomely.

The Americans, in particular, have expressed interest in our rocket development program, chemical warfare discoveries and atom bomb research. They have the metal, grain, wood, steel, and money to meet our requests. Negotiations are going on even now to have the leading researchers in those fields transferred to Arizona – a canton in the American desert. Of course, this will only be temporary, and all shipments will halt the moment our secondary industries get back on their feet. Solon also points out that a precedent was set in the last war whereby a defeated nation could ask for and obtain foreign aid from the victorious. We have no intention of being defeated but unnatural events have occurred before and we must keep all avenues open.

Cleisthenes has spent the last six months setting up the method whereby our Provisional Entente will move out of the shadows. On July 20, the present government leaders will be assassinated, leaving the country in a state of utter and complete turmoil. Thanks to the rapport between Cleisthenes and the present leader, these assassinations have the advantage of being conducted from the inside. The operatives have been given orders to spare no one who holds the rank or has ever held the rank of Minister. This is done purely for practical reasons – to prevent the possibility of the government's revival.

At the same time, all Generals hostile to our plan or who display any hesitation before joining us will meet the same fate. A trained assassin operates within the personal staff of every General and Minister. One month has been allowed for this, a month during which our people will get a further taste of chaos and the world will rub its hands furiously. But only for a moment. On August 20, Pericles is scheduled to make his first appearance since being banished to command the Western Wall. He is riding across the occupied territories in an open tank. His presence in the streets of the capital will undoubtedly serve to calm the people and make them realize a leader, a veritable saviour, is at hand. His magnetic personality requires neither fanfare nor forced demonstration.

However, just in case they are needed, Lycurgus will parachute a selected portion of his troops into the city, effectively surrounding it. Temporary headquarters for the new government will be the recently-vacated Collection Agency building (a touch of poetic justice). On August 29, Pericles is to make an appearance on the balcony wearing the new uniform which in modified forms will be adopted by all state functionaries – basic white Greek motif with slashes of red across the neck and stomach. The red is for hard lessons learned in the last twenty-five hundred years.

Immense celebrations have been prepared for that day and for the following octave. Pericles will walk among the people and allow them to touch him, revealing at the same time both legend and humanity. Solon declared himself against this on the grounds that many of the former leader's myrmidons might still be about. We are putting our faith in Pericles' charisma, along with the fact that, at the end of his walk, he will put to the torch all the records of the Collection Agency. It will be as if that abomination will never have existed, will have been obliterated off the face of the earth.

The most important and immediate effect of these letters and papers has been an increase in the powers of the Collection Agency. Most people, those with a clear conscience and a debt-free history, will be glad to know guns have been issued to the first-class Agents while now all have the right to search homes without a warrant. Several Agents, fearful of these very powers, have retired or been demoted. One of these was Claudius who, given an honourable discharge for performance of duties beyond the call, decided to join the Society of Jesus for a second time (or perhaps a third if one counts that fortuitous first time). He even visited Père Allemagne – the seminary being quite close – and was greeted with open arms as an old friend.

As well, extraordinary Agents have been assigned to uncover the instigators of the plot. Some are scouring the Ardennes Forest (with so far the only discovery being a bas relief sculpture, brought back to Agency headquarters as a keepsake). Others have infiltrated the wall as soldiers and military police. The arrest of Cleisthenes, most certainly identified as the Propaganda Minister, is imminent. By now, the rest of the traitors realize the letters and plans have been intercepted. We must act quickly before all evidence is destroyed. The dragnet closes in.

Two clues are permanent. The first is that, although it was mandatory once to learn some forms of ancient Greek at the Military Academy, not many officers could write it – and definitely not that known as "Linear B." Thus, Agents are presently examining the books and papers left behind at the Academy by the officer cadets. The second clue is that we have discovered in a post office in Caen a personal copy of Schiller's *Complete*. Nothing in it gives away the sender's identity but we are placing our faith in the poetic lady's love for Schiller. Sooner or later, in her desire to have her blood drained again and to feel the swoon of love palely loitering, she will claim it.

ITEM FOUR
A CONFESSION ~ AN OPERATION

Date Released: August 1, 1944
Author: Unknown
Circulation: Ministerial/Governmental/Collection Agency Executives
Type: Event Summary

*I*t was only a matter of time before the erudite conspirators were caught and brought to justice, each in his own way. Although, to a man, they denied any knowledge of the plot, the circumstantial evidence was overwhelmingly against them. All were in the right locations; all wrote that particular form of Ancient Greek among other long-dead languages; all were close friends who had gone to the Academy together. Thus, though no incriminating material was found, the logic was inescapable.

Lycurgus was arrested while in Caen trying to pick up Solon's gift. He seemed genuinely shocked when the Agents, posing as post-office clerks, surrounded him. At first, he berated them, calling them fools, screaming that he'd person-ally see them before a firing squad. Then, when he was brought before the Chief Agent for the section and shown the letters, he protested that they were forgeries. Yes, he had writ-ten similar letters but they contained nothing of shadow gov-ernments and plots, just friendly notes to his acquaintances. As a way to keep up his language skills – and those while still only a junior officer.

"You are ultimately disappointing," the Chief Agent said, holding Lycurgus' just-removed stars and shaking his head. "Very disappointing. A man of your rank and background is expected not to quibble with his captors. The Leader wishes to make it easy for you. A gun has been left in the cell. You have seen it, yes? It has one bullet. Why have you not taken the opportunity? Too squeamish? Well, then. A pill is provided with every meal. Are you saving them up for the pain of old age? Bah, it's almost enough to make me lose faith in your capacity to hatch such a plot."

Who then was this Lycurgus, this disappointment? None other than General Wilhelm Franck, in charge of northern wall defences and commanding a contingent of troops that numbered close to half a million. Continuing in his less than patrician bickering, he made no denial he could handle Greek – Greek poetry, in fact – but insisted it had been decades since he'd last used it to write anything. Nor did he have a typewriter with the Greek alphabet. And he claimed that the only Greek he'd spoken in the last year was at a feast in town when a seedy-looking officer had stood up and misquoted Sophocles. Franck had corrected him and the two had spent the rest of the night drinking, carousing, and playing out *Oedipus Rex*.

"Ah, but we're interested in all you classicists, are we not? All you aristocratic hobgoblins speaking languages that the rest of us thought long dead. His name, bitte?"

Franck hadn't bothered to ask. Naturally. That sort of camaraderie never does. Nor had he ever seen him again. To improve his memory, the Agency brought in his wife – more blanched than ever. The moment she saw Franck, she threw herself into his arms and blubbered how sorry she was. She didn't know it would end this way; she was only trying to do her duty, etc., etc.

"Your wife, sir," the Chief Agent explained, noticing the general's quizzical look, "has admitted to making the phone call that resulted in the interception of the courier. Patriotic, no? Not quite. She did it under threat of blackmail. Yes, my aristocratic friend with the leaden gauntlets. You should know you've been cuckolded and not by a classmate or one on equal social footing with you but by a common soldier at the wall. Though, to his credit, he is a fellow lover of Schiller and sea shells. Or so I'm told. At least, he was – until he decided to go for a swim and ran smack into one of our newfangled mines. How so? you ask. Why, he used his belt buckle to detonate it. Ingenious, no? In fact, the belt buckle was all that was ever found of him."

When Franck heard this, he reached over automatically for the gun. But it had been thoughtfully removed. No words were spoken but it was clear it would be returned only after he signed a confession implicating both himself and the others. He admitted his guilt but stopped at naming the others, claiming his honour as a soldier was at stake.

"That'll be enough for now," the Chief Agent said, smiling. "When honour's invoked, there's little even I can do. We'll round up the others ourselves."

And so the gun was restored to its rightful spot next to the general's bed. Franck, clutching it with both hands and forcing it into his mouth with a venom that would have done his Axis allies from the Land of the Rising Sun proud, blew off the back of his head. The Chief Agent could only sigh when told that, despite his honourable intentions, the general had botched it, had not done a clean job of it, had, in fact, bled for three days before merciful death took him. As a humanitarian gesture, his wife was allowed to nurse him, to hold his bloody, bandaged head on her lap.

Barely more than a vegetable, unable to control his bodily functions and constantly befouling himself and those around him, all his moments of consciousness were devoted to and concentrated on spitting in her face. In the end, the spit failed to reach her, dribbling down his chin instead and on to his disgraced uniform. When he finally expired, the Chief Agent allowed him, once more purely as a humanitarian gesture, to be buried quietly with an unmarked gravestone. His wife was left to wander the seashore like a wraith, scouring the empty bunkers in a mysterious quest that some saw as expiation and others as a search for the perfect love. As for Rollo, he too found himself on his own.

Solon proved the most difficult to ferret out. Neither army commander nor popular hero, his description matched that of a thousand other undistinguished civil servants, ratting their lives away beneath the grind of the state machinery. The Agents began by scouring his gift to Franck's wife, hoping for some hint of his identity. Several passages in *Wallenstein* were underlined in red. But that led nowhere. In fact, it was only with the apprehension of Franck and the subsequent examination of his private papers that enough information and clues came out to enable the Agency to narrow him down to one Johann Christoph Friedrich Krupp, a man of independent means and a hanger-on in government circles. In attempting to flee, he left behind several drafts of proposed laws, drafts which set in motion the machinery that would finally trap him as he tried to cross the Bodensee into Switzerland. As well, a specialized typewriter with ancient Greek characters was found in his room. That was definitely the clincher.

"Mr. Krupp," said his landlady on being questioned, "is a dangerous man. He's secretive and doesn't like to talk. Can a man be both silent and good? I don't think so. He had no friends. No, wait a minute. There was one – a shifty-eyed fellow with a sharp nose. He was the one who brought Mr. Krupp the typing machine. For a while, they were as thick as thieves, talking many nights till the sun came up. Whispering, actually, if you must know. Sometimes in this ugly language I couldn't make heads or arse of. One time, they got drunk together. Most stinking drunk. They began to dance like two clowns, going round and round till they fell down. Plop! That's when it happened. I had my eye glued to the keyhole and swear it's the truth. The nose of Mr. Krupp's friend got pulled away from his face – I swear! Like it was on a rubber band! Beneath it was another – an ugly hooked thing. He pushed the other nose back before Mr. Krupp noticed. I almost fainted, I tell you, and couldn't sleep for days. That's what you get for messing with the devil, I always say. The devil's nobody's pal."

Shortly after this incident, according to the landlady, the two friends split up. Krupp continued his night-long vigils, shuffling, arranging, and re-arranging a pile of papers left by this ex-companion. And typing away.

When Krupp found himself surrounded in the middle of the Bodensee, a spotlight on his rowboat and half-a-dozen machine guns trained on him, he shook violently and his teeth started a chatter that wouldn't stop until his demise. Having pity on him, one of the Agents decided not to shackle him for the train ride home. Krupp took the opportunity to strangle himself on the 'Pull-Cord,' sending the train screeching to a halt.

That Franck and Krupp should turn against their nation was not totally unexpected. Both had had their hopes and ambitions dashed: Franck, in his desire to be supreme commander and banished to the Wall instead; Krupp, in his realization he would never be more than a minor functionary. The Propaganda Minister, as well, had tasted too much power to be satisfied with second place on that elusive rung. But the revelation – through notes found on Krupp and other evidence of a circumstantial nature – that Pericles was none other than the glorious war hero Field Marshal Karl von Clausewitz caused ripples even in the highest circles.

So great was the shock that he was allowed to move about freely days after the others had been caught and done away with. (The Propaganda Minister's demise was particularly apt. Confronted with the evidence of his dastardly deeds, he was forced to chew on one of his own hate pamphlets – something about a Joseph So-und-So who'd been tortured by the Americans because of his pure Teutonic blood – that had been soaked in rat poison.) Two things were certain: no one would believe von Clausewitz capable of betraying his nation; and he must never be given the chance to appear in court lest his eloquence and bearing should win the day, should turn the tide against the government.

The solution came with the discovery he'd been under the weather for several weeks, listless and lethargic – extremely uncommon conditions for a man who'd sauntered through both desert and rain forest as if they'd been college outings to explore the Black Forest in search of fern and foxglove, broom and lupin. News was leaked on the state of his health. He was visited daily by a trusted doctor and close associate who was taken aside and given the option of choosing country over friendship – with a reminder, of course, that he had a lovely wife and five-year-old daughter back in Berlin. This doctor's duty was to misinform von Clausewitz as to the seriousness of the illness, which was nothing really but a bad flu.

"I'm sorry, Karl," the doctor said, not looking him in the eye, "but all I can do is recommend a period of total rest. Your body, weakened by old war wounds and a severe chest cold, is completely run down. There is the real danger that your continued frenetic pace will lead to permanent damage. I beg you to be particularly careful in the next month or so. Otherwise, you are liable to end up in a sanatorium. My only hope is that it isn't already too late."

But, of course, it was too late. Thanks to judicious injections, von Clausewitz weakened daily till he could no longer rise out of bed without help. Finally, noticing one day that von Clausewitz had barely the strength to discuss their favourite subject – the nature of a citizen's duty to his country in Plato's *Republic* – the doctor ordered him to be taken to a rest home. The tragic and fatal incident took place on the way there. Von

Clausewitz's personal bodyguards, following in their own car, saw the whole thing.

"The car," the senior bodyguard said in his report, "tripped a concealed wire and burst into flames. Field Marshal von Clausewitz was thrown clear of the blast but died of a broken neck on impact. Both the doctor and driver were charred beyond recognition."

The investigating committee linked von Clausewitz's death to the fact he had refused to go along with a plot to overthrow the government. It was the underground getting even, the traitors eliminating someone they couldn't turn. The incident served to rally the people. His fellow officers buried him symbolically at sea. Every concrete slit in the wall was draped in black. With the proper sense of decorum, his body was brought back to Berlin where, in an open tank stuffed with flowers, along streets thick with well-wishers, he rode triumphantly through the city, past the recently refurbished Collection Agency building, to the military cemetery. Where, according to the Leader's strict orders, a coffin filled with stones was lowered before a marble cross and avenging angel, and von Clausewitz's body hacked to bits and dumped out the back of a truck onto a back street of Berlin for the dogs and rats to consume.

If upon retirement Claudius had decided on any vocation other than the priesthood, the Collection Agency may not have allowed it to take place so easily. After all, here was a man crammed full of dangerous knowledge and bursting with secrets. As it was, his resignation was barely tolerated and a young Agent was assigned to him with orders to eliminate him if he so much as whispered a word of his previous activities. There was no question of concealment on this Agent's part and, to his credit, the Agent attempted none. In fact, the two of them developed a close friendship, going on long walks together and discussing everything under the sun other than Agency affairs. Occasionally, they would be joined by Père Allemagne.

The Agent inevitably ended up trapped between their gentle disputations. On these occasions, it crossed his mind, like it would have any conscientious Agent, that they might be talking in code, passing on secrets while pretending to be discussing the finer points of theology. How else could he explain such things as the ontological proof for the existence of God, the teleological argument by design, or the notion that a subtle difference separated the idea of an unmoved prime-mover and a self-moved one? But he kept his suspicions to himself. At least until further study and the breaking of the code. Besides, he had not been ordered to report back to the Agency; simply to erase Claudius if he should reveal any Agency secrets.

The environment was conducive to the development of a certain form of mental health. Daily, Claudius shucked off parts of his former identities. He put away, deep in a travelling trunk, every one of his disguises. Into mothballs and permanent storage went all manner of aliases, ID cards, moustaches, hairpieces, and noses (in particular, one very sharp one). With the help of the quiet surroundings where he could study or cultivate a garden, Claudius gradually developed the contemplative habit. Not that he was a mystic – far from it. Else he wouldn't have chosen to join the Society of Jesus. But the higher thoughts fascinated him and took his mind off what was going on in the world around him. His request to have Père Allemagne as his personal confessor was granted and Claudius found it pleasant to unburden himself once a week.

Not even the seminary walls, however, could keep out the news of major events outside: arrests of top army officers and government ministers, rumours of a plot to assassinate the Supreme Leader, mass suicides and full-scale rioting in the city centres, etc. The Agent tried to keep Claudius informed but the middle-aged seminarian showed no interest, except to make some cryptic remarks on the nature of guilt and innocence.

At the same time, those dedicated to his religious training realized he was keeping something from them, hiding something under a veneer of sweetness and compliance. They recognized it most strongly in the blood-red flowers he insisted on growing – the *Lobelia fulgens* and *Spekelia formosissima* – and in the topics he chose for his various theses, one of which he labelled *Torquemada: Saint in Devil's Clothing* or *No Tongs for the Memory*.

"There is something that keeps him from being one of us completely," wrote his immediate superior in a progress report (keeping as strong a tab on him as the Agent assigned to him). "Some secret or dab of guilt. Because of this, he is being prevented from attaining the highest spiritual level, that ultimate loss of self in the union of Christ. We must assume this is second nature for someone who has spent most of his life hunting down malcontents and misfits, the shadowy figures at the bottom of the social pool (scum some call it). In the long run, I believe this secretiveness and sleuth-like ability will guarantee him success as a member of our Society. After all, we do need new blood, a fresh approach. Someone who has tasted power and is secure in his use of it. With time and careful nurturing, he should go far. He is one we should hold onto with all our ability."

Claudius, not without guile in these matters, knew that the entire seminary waited for him to hurl himself to the ground and publicly confess, to scream out his sins in humble penitence while they cocked their ears to pick up dribbles of holy gossip. He also knew that, if anyone was to know what pricked his conscience, it wouldn't be the Jesuits. In his heart of hearts, he still pledged allegiance to his nation – and the Agency. Only Père Allemagne, because he was so straightforward, could talk to him with ease. And, for the same reason, gained no benefit from their conversations.

"All men are guilty," Père Allemagne would say when Claudius tucked into a *mea culpa* blood meal and vented about the evils he had done. "We must concentrate on charitable works and good deeds. You Jesuits are naughty children at heart, always thinking about some way or other to confuse people with your big, five-syllable words and fancy ideas. Look at the birds of the air and the creatures of the earth. Are they not happy? What does it matter if once you betrayed your friends or forged papers to catch debtors and traitors? Repentance is what God concerns Himself with. Repentance is what counts. That alone."

Claudius wished with all his heart that he could believe him, that he could let himself go, that he could negate himself.

"Love," Père Allemagne would say in his mysterious way, touching and tapping the side of his nose several times in succession. "That's the secret."

"I have never been in love," Claudius stated. "And now that I am in my middle years, I don't think I have the ability any longer to release myself into that maelstrom."

"Ah, but that's something no person can decide on his own. When it comes upon you, it is a light that floods all."

Claudius looked at him through the confessional grate. He saw the profile of someone who may never have experienced personal love, of the kind between two humans, but who nevertheless exuded something akin to the aura of sainthood. Claudius' heart overflowed with a new emotion for him: envy. For he knew that was unattainable for him – or would require too much stripping away to get to the core. Only to discover perhaps that there was no 'core.' That there might not be anything left but the pile of scrapings themselves.

ITEM FIVE
The New World ~ A Revamping

Date: May 1945
Author: Unknown
Circulation: Collection Agency Executive Committee
Type: Impressionistic Description/Setting The Ambiance

*T*hroughout the wild piano-playing night, middle-aged Claudius storms. He marches to and fro in his room, taking curt polite steps to one wall and then back again. Occasionally, he halts and looks at the paper in his left hand, holding it as far away as possible and squinting, for he has become somewhat near-sighted from too close a perusal of unilluminated medieval texts, lighted only from the phosphorescence of the gold flecks imbedded through the gilding process. The paper in his hand is an ad from a local newsletter, delivered weekly to the seminary:

> Claudius: With the termination of current hostilities, we must inform you that your complicity in the 'Greek Hoax Affair' can no longer be kept hidden. You should know that a warrant for your arrest has been issued by the provisional government. It is being held for the time being to allow you the opportunity to surrender. Due to your past work and services rendered, it will only be released 48 hours after this notice appears. Thank you for your time and consideration. Further contact through regular

channels is now no longer possible. But please note that this condition exists for all former and present Agents and will remain in force until arrangements can be made with whichever new power steps forward to take the reigns of government when the time to do so is deemed felicitous.

Sincerely as always,

The Collection Agency.

Claudius underlines 'reigns' – a common error – and then tosses the paper on the floor. Outside his room, the sky is brilliant with fireworks. Champagne bottles pop and foam at the mouth. Young men and women whirl through the streets, hugging, kissing, and pushing each other against walls with reckless abandon; tanks and armoured cars rumble; carbines and handguns are fired into the air; sad, shaven-headed creatures covered in tar and chicken feathers are dragged behind and beaten with twigs whose sap is still running.

In the recreation hall on the floor below him, he can hear the unaccustomed sounds of merriment as more and more of the Jesuits gather round the piano. He knows they are dancing with one another as they always do on such occasions, their skirts rising as Père Allemagne pounds out a hoarse tune of victory and liberty.

"God be blest!" Père Allemagne is shouting in his usual over-excited way. "God be praised! He has been our salvation in this supreme test of civilized man against the forces of barbarism."

"On the contrary, my dear Father," the head of the seminary, a thin, sharp-faced Jesuit with crow's feet eyes, says. "God has definitely kept His hands clean of this affair, allowing us to exercise all the tyranny of our free will. After all, that's what present-day war is about, isn't it? We strip each other to the bone and continue to flay away long after the enemy is helpless."

"God is compassionate," Père Allemagne insists, as if not really listening. "God is kind. He has vanquished the enemy in His inimitable way. The rest was punishment for our sins. It was a cleansing. A warning. A lesson."

"And what if the others had won?" another Jesuit chimes in, looking at the seminary head for approval.

"God would never have allowed that," Père Allemagne says with certainty. "The wicked shall be smote. And then forgiven. But never allowed to win. Remember: It is in pardoning that we are pardoned."

"Alas, dear Father Allemagne, kind, sweet and tender Father Allemagne. The Franciscans have always been better piano players than logicians."

"Where is Claudius?" Père Allemagne says, as if to prove the point. "I'm sure he would agree with me."

"*Non sequitur*," the Jesuits shout in unison, almost like a chorus. "*Non sequitur ad hominem* for certain." And the youngest, cheekiest one: "It's the lash for him."

Slumped astride the back of a wooden chair in Claudius' room and reflected uselessly in the mirror, the young collection Agent expires, gun held slackly in one hand, St. Thomas Aquinas' *Summa Contra Gentiles* slipping to the floor from the other. His mouth stretches open over one of the decorator studs that protrude higher than the chair back itself, as if his last act has been to suck on the little knob; his eyes stare straight ahead in puzzlement still (that unmoved prime-mover again); a trickle of blood below a powder-burnt hole mars his left temple. Claudius pries the pistol loose and throws it beneath the small bed on which he has tossed and struggled for the greater part of two years. It clangs against a large steamer trunk.

Père Allemagne, silenced in argument and running out of patriotic songs, starts on *Sur Le Pont D'Avignon*, carrying the tune as if it were Berlioz's *Symphonie Funèbre et Triomphale* suddenly gone berserk. The caretaker at the seminary, a lay brother emboldened by a bottle of the finest, and an unaccustomed sense of fraternity with events, shouts that the French Revolution has indeed returned and the people have once more won against superstition and slavery, tyranny, and oppression. For one frightening moment, only the crazed plinking of the piano can be heard in the deathly silence that follows this faux pas pronouncement, this reminder of complicity and betrayal. But then, perhaps because they are in a generous frame of mind, the members of the Society pass over the indelicacy (storing it nevertheless for future use) and festivities resume.

Claudius pulls out the trunk and opens it. Then he stands before the mirror, examining his face. He probes each wrinkle and crease, each hair that is slowly retreating in the already-lost battle with a receding hairline and eventual baldness. On the bureau sits a wig and a vanity case, much resembling those used by actors for their cosmetics. He lifts the body of the

Agent from the chair and drags it to the bed. Then, after a peremptory wiping of blood on the seat of the chair, he takes the Agent's place, opens the case, and begins to apply makeup. One by one, the wrinkles vanish, the creases fill out smoothly and the hair moves slowly forward over his forehead.

"Where's Claudius?" the head Jesuit shouts a few moments later, feeling his oats after the third or fourth glass of champagne. "Somebody get him down here. Let's hear what he has to say about it all."

"You mean, let's see where his loyalties lie."

Père Allemagne, out of songs and frankly bored with the discussion, volunteers. He shuffles heavily to his feet. The wine, although he's had barely two glasses, has made him tipsy and an idiot smile graces his face. He takes the stairs one by one, both feet to a step, holding on to the rail. Near the top, he lets go and swoons backwards as the entire group below him 'ooohs' and the lay brother rushes to his aid. But he manages to catch the railing and right himself.

"Faith, my children," Père Allemagne says, holding up his fingers. "The hand of God was upon my shoulder."

The head of the seminary turns to one side and makes a very remarkable noise, somewhat resembling a holy raspberry. The piano is taken over by an intense young man in rimless glasses, his back straight and his fingers trembling. All nervous energy. He approaches the keys gingerly as if expecting them to burn him or perhaps repulse him. When they don't, he starts up without any exercises. His notes are sharp, clear, logical, and biting – in total contrast to Père Allemagne's meandering lugubriousness.

"Being Christ's bridegroom can have its disadvantages, you know," one of the Jesuits says. "You stand by this frosted window and look out at the flying skirts, the joyful hands, the apple faces etched with pride. Even those who return to a cold bed and empty cupboards seem relieved and ready to take chances again."

"Ah, but we will have them again tomorrow," the seminary head says, his words now decidedly slurred. "We will have them again when they awake, their faces drawn with guilt and shame, their daily concerns coming again to the fore. We are lucky, after all, in being married to Christ. Our expectations are forever postponed."

While they talk, young adult Claudius puts the finishing touches to his nose. He polishes his shoes and straightens the vest from which suddenly dangles a heirloom watch. As he steps out the door, dragging the trunk behind him, Claudius surveys his room for one last time, lingering particularly over the Collection Agent back in the chair – and now suddenly himself a Jesuit, a middle-aged Jesuit with a receding hairline and a crooked nose. The smile on his face resembles that of Père Allemagne as the latter meets Claudius in the corridor.

"Ah, hello, young man. Leaving us, are you?" Claudius nods curtly, afraid to speak for fear of giving himself away to Allemagne's finely tuned ear. "Well, God bless you. A wonderful day for the free world in general and for young men in particular. No more war, eh? You can do what you fancy." He looks around. "Have you seen Claudius?" Claudius shakes his head. "So busy with his books I bet he doesn't even know. I think we'll have to put off the Judgement Day for that one, at least until he finishes his studies."

Père Allemagne suddenly feels even more tipsy. "Oops." He holds Claudius' arm to steady himself. Then he stares in amusement at him. "Say! Have you ever wondered what it would be like to be a priest? To take up the Shepherd's staff? Here, try on my collar for size." Claudius holds up his hands. "No, no. I insist. Every man, no matter what his calling, must taste once in his life the bliss and peace of priesthood."

Before Claudius has time to protest further or back away, Père Allemagne has removed the collar from his own neck and clipped it around Claudius'. Then he begins to clap and prance about like a monkey, delirious with his new method of conversion.

"There!" he says. "Isn't that a wonderful feeling? Why, it suits you to perfection. One would think you were born to the cloth. Ready to repeat: 'Do not wish to be anything but what you are, and be that perfectly.'"

Beads of perspiration break out on Claudius' forehead. The collar seems to be tightening; it is becoming hard to breathe. When he can take it no longer, he tears the collar off and throws it down. It flutters to the floor end over end.

"Oh dear," Père Allemagne says as he stumble-stoops to pick it up. "A little accident, eh? That's alright. We all have them, I guess."

But, when he looks back up, collar in hand like an offering, Claudius is no longer there, having taken the opportunity to slip away. Which is very fortunate indeed as he had been preparing, if everything else failed, to eliminate Père Allemagne with a swift blow to the hyoid bone.

"The wall proved a very limited defence," the seminary head is saying. "Our own General Ignatius would never have made such a mistake. You retreat and retreat, allow them to penetrate deep into your belly and then swallow them with one heave."

"What if it's Lent?" the priest near the window says with a guffaw, feeling a sudden unwelcomed twinge as he keenly observes a soldier manhandling a very willing young woman behind the woodshed.

"You could always convince your conscience that it doesn't really constitute food in the normal sense of the word."

Claudius feels a sudden sharp pang as he steps out the door, almost like homesickness. He strolls one last time through the gardens, stopping before his very own flowers, scarlet and brooding. The fireworks burst with renewed vigour above his head. He sees his fellow Jesuits – once a Jesuit always a Jesuit – through the window, their shadows moving, dancing, gesturing. For a moment, he thinks he sees someone waving from his room but that can't be. He puts the trunk in a wheelbarrow and leaves, pushing the barrow before him – like any other refugee.

✄✄

The Collection Agency's first hope had been that Claudius would rise to a position of influence within the Society, and then use that position to provide it with a direct line to the Vatican and a multi-national, captive market. When that goal was seen as unrealistic, due to turmoil caused by the end of the war (and the bad blood arising from the accusations and rumours of grim atrocities), it was decided to take up an entirely different direction and approach. Now, as several Agents track him westward across France – by foot, by horse, by train, by haycart, and again by foot – new plans are being formulated. For, as its enemies are soon to discover, the Agency, despite the fall of the government, is as strong as ever. Perhaps even stronger in the surrounding anarchy. It has undertaken, of its own initiative, to collect all war debts for the Allied Forces. As well, its thick dossiers have provided much of the material for those much-coveted and on-the-side-of-the-angels War Crimes probes. If you know where the skeletons are buried … and so forth.

The one thing on which the Agency finds itself unable to give any information is the aborted coup. Some investigators suspect that the men arrested and executed – the so-called Ancient Greek Connection – were innocent, victims of an elaborate frame. They also know that a real attempt at assassination and reform has failed because of beefed-up security around the Leader as a result of the Greek Connection Hoax. But that's as far as the investigation has gone, curtailed at the highest levels on both sides of the table.

At the same time, negotiations between the Agency and the Allies had started even before the wall had proved so easily penetrable. The Agency, in return for special favours and granting access to secret documents it had in its possession, requested a sphere of influence in America and permission to cross international borders without question. Crossing international borders was not something that could be granted, at least for the time being but, as a compromise, the Agency was given the right to collect all debts east of the Mississippi, as well as the ability to start its own banking concern. On the ground floor, as it were, in the edifice of the new world order. Although Claudius is as yet unaware of it, he has been chosen to head the new operation. No one else is anywhere nearly as qualified.

Thus, as the Agency formulates its new plans, consolidates old power and readies for the massive air lift to America (using funds from the Lend-Lease Program to re-establish its head-quarters in Seneca Falls, New York and later Chicago), Claudius rummages through the remains of the wall. It is like picking through his memories – especially one rusted-out crater of a bunker which he'd once visited as a bogus bedbug exterminator. There, he finds shells which he swears whistled tunes from Brecht's *Three-Penny Opera*, as well as copies of Spinoza and Freud, frayed, torn, and stuck together but still readable in places. As he leafs through *The Ethics*, several folded notes fall out. One is written on blue paper in a delicate feminine hand:

My darling, my love, my bedbug, my juicy hairy ape:
Never have I been happier or filled with more joy than during our time together, a time that is swiftly drawing to an end. Daily, I awaited my husband's departure from this imprisoning mansion so I could rush off to you. So I could lie beside you on your hard narrow bed. So I could be engulfed by your heat and the passionate grip of a love that knows no bounds. Despite the fact we can never see each other again,

for duty calls me, let us not forget one another, my furry seal, my sweet
lollipop, my damp lance. You have pierced me to the quick. Oh, I shall
never be the same again.
    Your Milk-White Maiden,
    Your Pale Lady in Distress
    P.S.: Please, please, please do not forget to mail those letters I left in
your charge. It is of the utmost importance.

Claudius thinks back on the intricacies of the Collection
Agency plan, the deftness and cleverness with which it has
been put in motion and then carried out. Once, there was
pride and a fair amount of hand-slapping and chest-beating,
emotions most suited to the battleground warrior in the heat of
battle. But now he feels mostly sadness – not for the Ministers
and Generals caught in the trap. No, they deserved all they got
and more, being guilty in thought if not in deed. He feels sadness for the fact that it has all come to an end, that it is all in
the past, that there is very little to look forward to from this
time onwards, that the peaks and valleys that have dictated his
life until now are being replaced by a flat entropic universe
where little happens to disturb the endless peace. The end of
history.

The other piece of paper consists of a series of sketches for
a bas-relief bust – of the Leader himself. Beneath the final one
is written:

    "Philhellene" (C.P. Cavafy)
    –Be sure the engraving is done artistically.
    [Seien Sie sicher der Stich ist gemacht künstlerisch.]

The expression grave and dignified.
[Das Ausdruckgrab und hat geehrt.]
The crown preferably narrow:
[Die Krone engt vorzugsweise ein:]
I don't care for the broad Parthian type.
[Ich pflege mich der breite Parthian nicht.]

As well, the bunker is littered with enemy propaganda pamphlets. Claudius reads with tell-tale interest the alleged atrocities described therein. How millions have been herded into cattle cars and brought to God knows where for God knows what purpose, how experiments with still-living humans have disguised sadistic pleasure under the panoply of scientific interest, how minds have been pried open with the most subtle and unsubtle of crow bars. Knowing that statistics dull the senses, some of the pamphlets employ a more personal tack:

Joseph So-Und-So, loyal citizen of the Fatherland, was taken away recently before the incredulous eyes of his wife and daughters.

(Here, two pictures: one of a smiling man in Bavarian halter and shorts, looking beyond the photograph at something that has made him smile; the other of a near-skeleton with numbers across his chest and a huge scar along the scalp line.)

From a healthy butcher and contented family man, he has been reduced to little more than skin and bones. In fact, it might be better if he were dead as the picture doesn't reveal all the torture heaped on him. Why? For crimes

against the fatherland? For collaborating with us, the enemy? For traitorous
actions too foul to mention? No, my patriotic defender. Only because …

Claudius tires of reading and, besides, none of this can possibly be true, from one side or the other. Simply typical wartime propaganda. Instead, he gazes through the slit in the bunker, using his new-found books to achieve the necessary height. On the water, minesweepers search for the last of the mines while fishing boats bob impatiently in port, hoping to at long last resume their livelihood. For a moment he thinks he sees a woman shimmering on the water, a woman in a white nightgown, floating just above the water. But then the image vanishes. Instead, a large and immaculately-shaped German shepherd races along the shore. It enters through one side of his line of vision and is on the verge of vanishing at the other. But it never makes it all the way across. Instead, the air cracks twice with a sound all too familiar during wartime and it pitches … stumbles … falls forward in the sand, hurtling for a few metres more before coming to a halt right at the edge of Claudius' sight. A soldier carrying a carbine leaps over the top of the bunker. When he arrives near the dog, it makes a weak effort to spring up, lifting itself momentarily by its back legs before collapsing again. The soldier aims the rifle, fires, and blows off half its head. Then he turns towards the bunker and shouts above the wind.

"Dead dog, sir. All clear."

"Positive?" shouts back a cracked but authoritative voice, the type of voice used to having instructions followed to a tee.

"Not moving, sir."

"That's not the same as being sure. Make sure."

"Yes, sir!"

The soldier shoots the carcass again, sending up a spray of sand in a V-shape opposite from the trajectory of the bullet.

"That does it, sir. Dead dog."

The second soldier comes down towards the dead dog. Claudius can see he is a high-ranking officer, a general perhaps, judging from the three silver stars.

"I hope so," he says. "I wouldn't want that enemy animal jumping one of my men from behind. Wouldn't look good, would it?"

"Not at all, sir."

"Bad for morale."

"Most definitely, sir."

Taking the hint, the soldier fires yet one more time, propelling the remains of the dog a few more metres down the beach. He places a foot beneath it and flips it over onto its back. Claudius can see the tongue sticking out the side of its mouth, like a red flower bursting forth.

"Dead as dead can be, sir. Positively. No doubt about it."

"Don't get me wrong, soldier," the general-type soldier says, sighing and looking out across the water, with an almost sensitive expression on his craggy face. "I love dogs. I really do. Especially intelligent and obedient dogs. Dogs that are good at following orders, like I bet this fellow here was. But it can't be helped. The circumstances of war, you know. I took my beloved Japanese spaniel out into the backyard and shot him right after Pearl Harbor. Between the eyes. Couldn't very well risk having a spy in the house, now could I?"

"No, sir! Did you get another one, sir?"

"What! Another slant-eyed gook!"

"No, sir. Another dog?"

The two soldiers continue the track started by the dog, and quickly move beyond Claudius' ability to see from his slit-hole vantage point.

"Damn right! Scottish terrier. A real ratter. First animal out of the landing craft at Juno. He raced right out and latched onto the leg of the enemy. Just like I trained him."

Claudius assumes they continue to walk and talk once they vanish but of course he can't be really sure of it. Instead, he leans against the wall of the bunker and slowly slides down to the floor.

On the initial part of the voyage to the New World, Claudius stays mainly in his cabin. When not practicing his English or reading a book on grammar (Mencken's *The American Language, 4th edition*), he paces from bunk to door and back, feet apart to balance himself against the North Atlantic swells. The effort needed to stay upright prevents a flight into more abstract and thus more dangerous thought. It would be an appropriate time to reflect on the mechanics of divine intervention in the world: how, on several occasions, the military police had been closing in and then suddenly turned away to pursue someone else; how, even more amazingly, he'd found a wallet stuffed with money, a passport and steamship tickets just as he was about to turn around and head back to Berlin; how he'd been able to use the picture in the passport to make himself its spitting image. Or is it that the passport picture already resembles him oh so very closely that all he needs is a bit of a touch up? No, that's not something he is willing to entertain at this time.

But it isn't reflection Claudius wants. It isn't introspection or internalization, let alone speculation. He longs for one thing and one thing only − for confession. Simply a habit, of course, made enjoyable by Père Allemagne's short breath and Solomon-like advice that just barely missed the mark with quotes like: "Start by doing what is necessary; then do what's possible; and suddenly you are doing the impossible." He tries the Protestant approach by opening the porthole and shouting out his sins directly to God: *Forgive me, God, for I have sinned. I have sinned grievously, have committed crimes against both man and nature. Are you out there? Are you listening? Do I get absolution? Is there a direct line?* Or perhaps something more Jesuitical: "What seems to me white, I will believe black if the hierarchical Church so defines."

Try as he might, it falls flat, falls into unbelief and doubt, tasting of nothing but saltwater spray. How can anyone take that sort of thing seriously? he finds himself thinking. How can anyone so misjudge human nature as to place any trust whatsoever in the ability of a person to do the right thing without anyone making sure that the person is doing the right thing? He thinks back on the schoolmaster who had once handed him a stick and told him to go into the closet and punish himself. Punish myself? Claudius bursts out laughing at the memory. Whack! Whack! Whack! Against the clothes closet wall. A verisimilitude of painful screams. No, better yet were the whacks against the winter boots of his classmates: That made the kind of moaning fleshy sound that really attracted God's forgiveness. Ha, ha.

His private joke is interrupted by an almost inaudible knock and the slipping of a fancy, gold-embroidered note beneath his cabin door:

Dear Fellow Traveller:

It is with profound and delightful pleasure that the Wands, Martin and Alba, cordially invite you to an escargot and white wine party. Time: Ce soir. Midnight and thereafter. Place: The Main Deck Dining Rooms A & B. Reason: A chance to get better acquainted, to re-discover moonlight and romance on the high seas, to celebrate our progress towards the New World. Dress: Come as you will, Costume, Casual, or Formal. No RSVP necessary. Just show up!

Claudius tosses the note on his bunk and returns to pacing. He is somewhat irritated by this invitation. Just because he's given up the priesthood doesn't call for a complete return to that filthy, scum-laden tidal pool some call society. And escargots to boot! He recalls vividly how one of the Parisian debtors had, during the war, tried to settle his accounts with several boxes of caviar, which for some reason always seemed to go hand in hand with escargots.

"Sir," the recently nabbed debtor called out as Claudius removed yet one more piece of his face, thus making him look less and less like the debtor's future son-in-law, the resemblance that had gained him entry in the first place. "Sir, I assure you it is worth more, much more, than the debt. The caviar is the black variety. Smuggled from Russia at great risk in the stomach of a dead mule."

"It is the Agency's considered policy to accept nothing but hard currency with the occasional allowance for non-comestible goods in trade. In fact, you should be thankful francs are still allowed."

"Of course, of course. I can see the logic in that. After all, no one desires rooms full of caviar and such. Francs neither, for that matter. But these are, you must agree, exceptional circumstances. Surely even you can understand. I have nothing but caviar – and … and a few philosophy books."

"Books? Philosophy books?"

"Yes – I mean no! I've sold them all. For a moment I'd forgotten I'd sold them all."

"We accept books as payment in barter. If they are neither subversive nor too new. So if you wish to retract your previous statement which appears to have been made in haste …"

"Yes, yes, that's it! They are sub – I mean, of course not! How silly of me." He takes a deep breath and exhales as if he doesn't really want to. "They are mainly, if you must know, on the old Greek democracies. Nothing new or subversive. Nothing subversive or new. Tales of the Greek democracies and their famous leaders. Some Ancient Greek language lessons. Moral instructions suitable for upper grade school children. Comparing and contrasting Sparta and Athens."

"Splendid. I'll take those on the assumption they are what you say they are, of course. The boys back at the Agency can always use a good fairy tale to keep up their spirits."

Claudius sighs at the memory. It all seems oh so long ago now. Everything was laid out and orderly then, even in the midst of chaos and world war. There was an anchor. Everything had its place in the carefully planned ledgers, the hand-written spreadsheets listing every single detail of every single person in the nation, be that person good citizen, traitorous double Agent or genetically impure and destined for liquidation. And the debt collection! Oh, the debt collection. Such efficiency. Such statistical compliance. Would such a time ever come again? Claudius fears not. He has been informed that the New World is all about so-called individuals, freedom, choice, the power to decide on one's own how to conduct one's life with as little government and bureaucratic interference as possible. Is there room in this vast circus of individual movement and survivalist mentalities for group action? For anomalies such as collection agencies? He doesn't think so. No matter what his instructions might be.

But … he must make the best of it. He reaches down and opens his travelling trunk. Tucked into one of the side pockets is a very official looking letter of authorization, identifying him as a high-level member of the Collection Agency Executive Committee (even if only recently promoted through the age-old process of attrition). And a note of introduction to Prescott Bush at the Union Banking Corporation in New York with authority to access five million in credit on 24 hours notice. This is to be seed money for the creation of a combination lending and debt collection institution to be named as Claudius sees fit – and with Claudius as the first director.

Claudius is thinking very much of the folly of such an enterprise in a place where the Agency has no infrastructure whatsoever (and perhaps the more sane option of simply taking the funds and vanishing into the jungles of South America where, as far as he knows, the former Archbishop [Cardinal Most Holy?] of Nice might still be lurking) when there is a sharp rap on his cabin door. And then another.

"Yes?" he asks, replacing his letters of introduction and authorization.

"Steward, sir. To refresh your bed."

Claudius opens the door to let in the clad-all-in-white steward who is pushing a cart before him with fresh bed linen piled atop. He notes that there is something vaguely familiar about the man but attributes it to the fact that a steward's uniform makes them all of a type, as it were.

"Good afternoon, sir," the steward says. "I hope I'm not disturbing you."

"Not at all," Claudius says, turning and busying himself with other matters. "We all have our tasks to perform. That is how a well-functioning society works."

The steward pushes the cart forward and then stops almost directly in front of Claudius.

"Yes?" Claudius says, looking up to notice the steward staring directly at him in a bold and unblinking way. In a very un-steward-like way.

"You don't remember me, do you?" the steward says.

Claudius looks at him again, notes that his name tag reads: "Schweik," and then shrugs: "I'm sorry. Am I supposed to know you? I don't recall having met you before."

"Belt buckle," Schweik the Steward says cryptically.

"My God!" Claudius says in sudden recognition and taking a step back. "But you … you were killed … in a mine explosion … all they found …"

"… was the belt buckle. Yes. The officially non-existent belt."

"So …" Claudius looks around, as if the explanation were floating in the air, were something he can pluck like a fruit.

"Ah … one of my less fortunate mates … a poor swimmer … especially weighed down that way. He really admired that belt."

"And … what brings you here?" Claudius asks, regaining some of his confidence. Or at least putting on an air of confidence. "What is it you want?"

"Well," Schweik says, sitting on the bed, "to tell you the truth, I wasn't really sure when I knocked on your door. It is as if I was walking about in a trance ever since I spotted you coming aboard. In a dream really. Or maybe nightmare."

He leans over to peer into the still-opened trunk, reaching in to finger some of Claudius' clothing, mostly consisting of bits and pieces designed to be slapped on in order to quickly change his appearance.

"Ever the master of disguise, eh, Claudius? Ever ready to flee into the nearest church. Or jump into the nearest manhole."

"Part of my trade," Claudius says, as he pulls closed the lid of the trunk, causing Schweik to retract his fingers. "As you are so well aware, some of the people with whom I had business dealings would never let me approach close enough to conduct those dealings if they would come to recognize me." He holds out his hands. "So, one needs to learn to adapt – and do so as quickly as possible."

"Yes, yes. I understand completely. Military bed bug exterminators, priests, mothers grieving over their infants, high-ranking government officials … Quite a versatile and expansive acting range."

"Thank you," Claudius says with a curt bow and a tapping of the back of his heels. "But you have as yet not told me what it is you want. Why you are here."

"Ah, how quickly they forget. The cruel ones of science. The ones who treat the little ones like experiments. The ones who play around with us from on high. The …" He stops and takes a deep breath. "Let me not beat about the bush."

"No, please don't. By all means."

"Bad enough you hounded and tormented me. I could take that. But then you started to do the same with the only person who ever cared for me."

"The woman you loved?"

"My mother. My sainted mother."

"Your mother?"

"You killed her. You tracked her down and wouldn't leave her alone. You used her as a pawn in one of your games. And then threw her away. She died because of you. She couldn't take your hounding anymore." His voice cracks and he has difficulty holding back tears. "She died for nothing. No one should die for nothing."

"I'm sorry," Claudius says. "I guess we were talking about two different women."

"What? I'm talking about my mother. You tracked her down in Königsberg. You searched our house for that accursed belt. You told her you would be back again and again until you found that belt."

"Yes, I remember. You can imagine my disappointment when the Königsberg your mother lived in was not the city that gave birth to Goldbach, Hoffmann, Hilbert, and dear old Kant."

"I'm talking about my mother, damn you!"

"So … what now?" Claudius says. "What's done is done and I personally think that this conversation has been exhausted."

"Not quite," Schweik says, pulling out a gun from beneath the bed linen and waving it about.

"Now, we're getting down to the nitty-gritty," Claudius says. "A Walther Spreewerke P-38 9mm pistol. Excellent choice. First rate." He holds out his arms as if preparing to receive a bullet. "If I'm to die, at least it'll be at the hands of a patriot with a patriot's favourite weapon. And someone, I trust, who will allow me to say my prayers before sending me off into oblivion."

Schweik stands and, from a metre or so away, aims the pistol at Claudius' temple.

"Yes," he says. "Say your prayers. To whichever god you pray. I haven't been able to figure that one out yet."

There is silence for a moment or two. Claudius stands extremely straight and still, looking directly ahead. Schweik tries to steady his gun hand. But he is finding it difficult. A small alarm clock on the headboard ticks away the seconds.

"Come," Claudius says, squaring his shoulders even further. "Pull. Squeeze. Act. Commit. Do it now. You will not get this opportunity again."

But Schweik's hand refuses to steady itself, even when he uses the other one for a two-handed grip. After a dozen or so seconds and with a wrenching motion, he lowers the gun, lets it drop on the floor and seats himself on the bed, head in his hands.

"I'm nothing but a coward," he says, breaking down into tears. "I can't even shoot my worst enemy. The man who was responsible for my mother's death."

"Well, at least you don't hold me responsible for the death of your one true love."

"My one true love?" He scratches his head. "I don't think I've ever had one of those."

"Oh well, there's still time," Claudius says, sitting down beside him and placing one arm around his shoulder. "But you shouldn't be so hard on yourself. You're a decent and honourable man. A soldier, correct?" Schweik nods. "Soldiers are not trained to shoot unarmed civilians."

"I've never shot anyone," Schweik says. "Armed or unarmed."

"You'd rather read poetry, no? Schiller? Goethe? Heine?"

"Read poetry?" Schweik says, with a puzzled look.

"Shells, then?" Claudius gets up and goes to his trunk. "Like this?" He pulls out a large coffee table style book. "*The Collector's Guide to Seashells of the World.*" He opens and places it in front of Schweik. "Look at this! The Pacific Murex Ramosus! Amazing, isn't it?"

"What are you talking about?" Schweik says, becoming agitated. "Are you making fun of me? What do I know of shells? I barely made it out of the third grade."

"No, no," Claudius says, replacing the book in the trunk. "Just one of those fantasies of mine. Just like true love and the study of elasmobranch fishes. No offense intended." He sits back down and turns Schweik's hands towards him, palms up. "I can see that you're an honest labourer. Brick layer? Shoemaker?"

"Quarry man. On the outskirts of town."

"Aha!" Claudius jumps up. "A rock splitter. An artist in stone."

"Artist? I don't think so. Just a lot of hard work."

"Hands of thunder, eh?" He snaps his fingers. "I have it! Tell me, have you thought about what you want to do once we reach the New World?"

"I hadn't really thought about it. No plans other than getting my revenge on you."

"Bodyguard," Claudius says.

"Bodyguard?"

"Yes. Praetorian. Beefeater. Yeoman." Claudius leans down, picks up the pistol and hands it back to Schweik. "Here, my good man. It appears to me that, in this New World of ours, a bodyguard will come in quite handy amid all those rampant individuals pursuing happiness. Besides, how can someone ever hope to be a respectable banker without a guardian ... protector ... shielder to watch one's back?"

"A bodyguard?" Schweik says again, looking at the pistol.

"Yes," Claudius says. He opens the trunk one more time and pulls out an envelope which he hands to Schweik. "Here you go."

Schweik dumps the envelope onto the bed and a passport falls out.

"What the—"

"Diplomatic pass," Claudius says. "You won't even have to go through customs." He pats Schweik on the shoulder. "The least I could do."

"I don't know what to say," Schweik says, head slightly lowered. He pauses, then clears his throat. "I have a confession to make ... That belt—"

"Stop right there," Claudius says, holding up his hand. "Say no more. I want to hear nothing about that belt."

"But—"

"No!" He places his hands on his hips and stands before Schweik. "We are turning over a new leaf this day. The past is dead. What took place between us is dead. What was left unfinished is dead. We are as two newly-risen phoenixes. We remember nothing! Repeat after me: 'I remember nothing!'"

"I remember nothing."

"Again. With enthusiasm."

"I remember nothing!"

"Good," Claudius says. "Now remember that!"

Somewhere on the liner, a piano breaks into sporadic music. At first, there is no particular form to it. Simply a chaotic rumble. A reverberation. But then Claudius recognizes a familiar tune, *Sur Le Pont D'Avignon*, amid the random tinkling.

"You know," he says, "I was all for avoiding this ... this cookhouse party. But I've changed my mind. You hear that, Schweik? The music has altered my emotional equilibrium. Or maybe it was the combination of your appearance and the music. In any case, here's your chance to show me what you've got. Come, give me a hand."

Still somewhat stunned at the turn of events, Schweik rises slowly from the bed, looks at the gun in his hands and slips it into his pocket.

"I'll need a holster," he says, as if he has made a decision about something. "If I'm to be a proper bodyguard, I'll need to be able to react quickly."

"Most definitely," Claudius says, reaching into the trunk for some appropriate party attire. "First thing we get after stepping off the ship in New York. Now, help me put this on."

Claudius dresses in the best suit available – the jacket and trousers from his Society of Jesus uniform, omitting the collar naturally – and, with Schweik right behind him, looking right and left, steps out into the corridor. It is early evening, nearing sunset. The water is red on the horizon. *Incarnadine*. The world's skin tone.

"Amazing," Claudius says. "Schweik, I feel lucky tonight."

"Lucky?"

"Lucky in love."

From cabins all around them, couples emerge, arm in arm, dinner-jacketed, white-gowned, carnations in lapels, perfumed and intoxicating. People smile at Claudius as they squeeze by; necklines plunge before his eyes; piano keys like teeth chatter. Someone nearby pops a champagne bottle, hands out glasses, and offers the spilling contents to him. The bubbles prick his nose but he forces himself to take a swig. Necks arch up and curve away into dazzling jewels; top hats snap open in the velveteen blackness. Cigar smoke curls to the ceiling. *On the thighs of virgins.* He looks behind him: Schweik also has a champagne flute in his hand and a slinky-gowned woman on each arm. Claudius gives him the thumbs up.

"This way to the Wands!" yells a clownish-looking man waving a staff at the end of which is carved a ram's head. "Don't permit yourself to miss the fun! No substitutes should be accepted! The party of the century, putting to shame anything cobbled together by those wannabes, the Rockefellers, the Morgans, the Hearsts."

Parting the people with his staff, he charges, bulls, slices his way to the front. Once there, he begins to skip furiously from side to side, lifting his knees high into the air – much like the leader of a brass band at a parade. Without a moment's hesitation, the followers, including a particularly enthusiastic Schweik, take up the beat and the metal corridor rings with boisterous joy. They dance their way towards the main dining room, Claudius swept along with them, feeling the supple, yielding bodies press against his.

Their path leads them momentarily out on deck. The North Atlantic rolls clear and caustic, a full moon reflects shivering in the ship's wake. Red has turned to silver. Then, after this captivating glimpse, the line arches back into the corridor where the lights have been dimmed by some unknown purveyor of atmosphere. Amid the dark turmoil, the rubbing, the perfumed heat, the nose-flanging cigar-smoke, the knot in his stomach, Claudius reaches for the body he's been smelling and desiring ever since he left the cabin. It yields effortlessly as he presses it to the wall and they writhe together, his tongue darting like a wild bird in its mouth, the sweet taste of lipstick, the mashing of groins and thin hip bones, tiny breasts, vulval delights. Immediately, Schweik is beside them but then turns away when he realizes there is no danger. Claudius holds the body close to his, as if he has known her all his life. As if they are somehow old friends.

"What a surprise," he whispers in her ear. Nibbles at her ear.

"Here we are! Here we are! Here we are!" the ram's-head man shouts. "The Promised Land! Or at least the portal! Let it part!"

The dining-room doors are held together for a moment and then thrown open – to belly laughs and cheering, to toasts, to the squealing of … to silence, to thin, high-pitched wailing, to the depths of mourning. The entire party comes to a stop at the doorway, staring in disbelief at what they see. Or think they see since the only light comes from two huge candles at the far end of the room. The intervening space is filled with a hot steam rising to sting the eyes, as one might imagine floating in the space above the Styx.

Out of respect, Claudius releases the body beside him. An old woman with silver hair and a glint of diamond tiara, seated in a wooden chair with her back to them, turns briefly their way. Not for a moment does she halt her wails. A younger woman in a sequined dress sits beside her. She doesn't move a muscle. Claudius appreciates the candlelight on her neck, reflecting the soft white flesh and the golden down. Suddenly her head heaves, lurching the upper part of her body forward.

An open coffin stands on two sawhorses before them. In it, the face of a middle-aged man is profiled amid a garland of red roses. The clownish-looking person with the ram's head has already rushed up to the coffin in exaggerated pantomime. He hovers over the body, head to one side, wiping huge luminous tears from his eyes. Then he leans down and, with his hands spread, kisses the man on both cheeks. The rest of the revellers, not quite sure what to do, creep along the walls and take on the guise of mourners as well, some of them tucking in their breasts, buttoning their shirts, and pinning the slits in their dresses. Or turning their white tuxedos inside out. So well does each play the part that, when the old woman stands up to receive condolences, the party-goers file past one by one, shaking hands and heads like long-time acquaintances of the newly-deceased. The daughter (or so everyone assumes) never turns, her grief so great her thin body is racked with constant heaving.

The steam increases in strength, making it devilishly hot and clammy. Claudius waits his turn, too late now to sneak away. He leans against the dining-room wall and listens to the piano. It seems to be coming from the other side of the hall and just slightly above. The captain perhaps in his private stateroom? The music is now polished and sure of itself, mastering *Feu d'artifice* with ease. He looks out the porthole at the brilliant moon and the Big Dipper, decanting on to the ship like a shadowy carafe.

"Ah, Father," the old woman says as she takes his hand, "could you say a little something? A proper send-off into the other world? It would be greatly appreciated."

Is he that obvious? He looks down at himself. Schweik, standing to one side, smiles at him and urges him on. The clownish-looking man starts to nod frantically and points at the body while the daughter continues to heave.

"I'm not—" Claudius starts to say.

"We're not of the same faith. Yes, Father," the old woman says painfully, using her handkerchief to wipe something from his lips. "But is that important at this time? You look like such a good man. I'm sure the portion of God we don't share wouldn't mind. And the part we do would be most grateful."

Claudius must think of something to say. By now, he has tacitly admitted his priesthood. He feels as if all eyes are on him save those of the daughter. He looks around. The woman beside him, shrouded in darkness, leans forward and, pretending to whisper in his ear, sticks her tongue in instead. He can feel his own tongue swelling in his mouth, threatening to explode between his teeth, threatening to come out in an obscene gesture that would expose his perfidy to everyone in the room. The old woman squeezes his arm. Tears stain her dress and his suit. The gowns swish like ghosts around him, urging him on.

"Give them your blessing," the woman beside him whispers, voice calm and reassuring.

Claudius raises his hand in a tremulous sign of the cross, making every effort to concentrate on something else. The flaxen moon flooding the porthole directly above a woman's bowed head; the candles, thick and warm and oozing wax; the innumerable debts he's squared away; the clownish man eating roses with a soft, chewing sound; the piano playing *La mer*.

Claudius racks his brains for something appropriate to say. Then, thinking back, he gets it. It comes to him. He starts to recite:

Oh God, the Creator and Redeemer of all the faithful: grant to the souls of thy servants and handmaids the remission of all their sins, that they may obtain by our pious supplications the remission they have ever hoped for. Who livest and reignest.

May the angels lead thee into paradise; at thy coming may the martyrs receive thee, and bring thee into the holy city, Jerusalem. May the choir of angels receive thee, and with Lazarus, once a beggar, mayest thou have eternal rest.

"Amen!" exclaims Mr. Wand, sitting up in the coffin as the lights burst forth from all directions to reveal tons upon tons of escargots writhing in a sea of garlic sauce.

Mrs. Wand throws off her mourning clothes. Beneath them, she is wearing a low-cut diaphanous gown sliced down the back to below the upper portion of her buttocks. And her daughter finally turns, her face distorted with laughter.

Claudius stands there in a state of paralysis as Mr. Wand walks up to him and gives him a friendly clap on the back. But not before Schweik moves forward just in case.

"Congratulations on your most prestigious appointment," says Mr. Wand. "I'm sure you'll do your country – and ours – proud. And what better way to celebrate than with a costume party? So, let's party!"

Mr. Wand grabs his wife and lifts her across the dance floor. One of her breasts plops out. He leans down and licks her nipple as she tosses her head back in delight. The far end of the stateroom opens up and a band appears on a circular dais – four swinging, swaying jazz musicians wearing outlandish white zoot suits and fedoras. At first, Claudius can't make out who they are. But, as the dais swings his way, he recognizes them as if in a fog and the names roll through his mind: the Propaganda Minister, Franck, Krupp, von Clausewitz … the whole gang. They smile and wave at him before returning to their playing. Two girls, identical twins attached by some kind of living, breathing cord, belt out *Murder, She Said!* into a pair of fancy mikes. The clownish-looking man is beside himself with glee and keeps bursting out laughing while clapping his hands.

Now visible under the bright spotlights, it is a very pale, very skinny, very flat-chested and hollow-eyed woman with smeared purple lipstick who pushes up against Claudius. She is holding a bust under one arm. It is a bas-relief of Claudius. Everyone cheers as the two of them kiss, exchanging once again their pulsing tongues.

"Welcome to the New World, mein Kommandant," she says in a husky voice as she hands him the bust. "Together, we will go far, you and I."

"Thank you, Père Allemagne," Claudius says before he can stop himself.

ITEM SIX
In The New World ~ A Fragment

Date: Unknown
Author: Unknown
Place: Unknown

*A*s he lies in bed, curled up like a question mark against his partner, Claudius feels the most iridescent urge for home. Except that he no longer has a home. The stars are different here. Brighter than life, full of explosions and a cryptic energy that constantly threatens to … There are things here that make no sense to him, phoenix from a shell-shocked and crumbling universe. He understands only the order that grew from hob-nailed boots and guilt, from hammer blows to the back of the head. Here, people scuttle about as they wish … make their lives below the radar. The dancers … oh, the dancers … It is a giant ship cruising through eternally calm waters. Even the rats and the cockroaches are a dying menace, driven out by sub-sonic booms only they could hear, the Pied Piper of Post-Modern Technology.

Claudius doesn't know what he would do without Père Allemagne curled up beside him – a light that floods all … or without Schweik sitting on a stool against the bedroom door … it is for them now that he feels he must present himself at the Union Banking Corporation … to start anew … to recreate a piece of the old world …

"If you are going to go through with this," Père Allemagne says, whispering into his back before kissing it, "you must give it a name. That's always the first step. Isn't that right, Schweik?"

"Yes," says Schweik, looking up from his *All Select* comic book starring Captain America. "If you say so."

"No," Claudius says, sinking back into his question-mark pose beside Père Allemagne. "I will not give it a name."

… And so it comes to pass that Claudius does not give it a name … He hands his authorization and letters of credit to the director of the Union Banking Corporation and walks out.

"They'll come after you," Père Allemagne says. "They'll demand their pound of flesh. Right, Schweik?"

"Yep," Schweik says, trying to practice his colloquial American. "You bet."

"Perhaps. But they know what I have and coming after me is the surest way of letting the cat out of the bag. Besides, they'll be too busy trying to find ways to get even richer than they already are and trying to take over the known universe to worry about the likes of me."

[There follows one last cryptic note]

… "Mountain … sky … lanterns … truth … the art of shelling beans … great reeds whistling in the night wind … turn out the lights …"

TRANSLATOR'S
CONCLUDING REMARKS
On Closing The Files

*G*iven the age of the main protagonists at the time the incidents in these files took place or are alleged to have taken place, it is safe to assume that, unless true werewolves or vampires, they are no longer with us. Or at the very least, Claudius and Père Allemagne, who were already well into middle age, are long gone while Schweik, if still with us, would be in his mid-to-late 90s. And nothing is known of them beyond what appears here.

In fact, there is but one single recorded entry found at the NatSoc Workers' Bank – presumably an ironic title given it by the director of the Union Banking Corporation who seems to have had a fondness for doing business with fascists – that refers to the files or the three main protagonists. And that only obliquely. That was back in 1946, indicating only that a certain Father Laudamus had rented out the safety deposit box in which the files were subsequently found.

It would thus seem that the game of cat and mouse, which Claudius delighted in playing, meant placing the dangerous evidence right under the very noses of those who would have slit his throat without a second thought had they known. Judging from the final fragment, it appears Claudius decided he was no longer cut out for the work of collection Agent and wished for a more private life, one in which he could pursue other interests. I would be very keen to discover what those other interests finally led him to do and/or become. If there is anyone out there who can enlighten me on this point, I would be eternally grateful.

In any case, one thing is abundantly clear: If Claudius thought that his abdication would lead to the collapse of the system he no longer wanted any part of, he was sadly mistaken. While the notion of a centralized Collection Agency under the auspices of the government bureaucracy never did take hold in the New World (given its penchant for both pseudo- and uber-individualism), the parallel notion of handing out money to its citizens in order to keep them permanently in debt became part and parcel of the fabric of that society. And Claudius himself would not have lived long enough to witness the start of the process of the slow teetering over and implosion under its own bloated carcass of that society, making the collection of much of the debt impractical and unnecessary.